I0727832

Where Worlds Avoid

Dan Treacy

Copyright © 2022
All Rights Reserved

Table of Contents

For Dorothy.

Love and laughter is everything, always.

About the Author

Dan Treacy is a solicitous man and a political animal who uses his time to educate others around him about the ways of the known and unknown world. His dream of equality and peace remains in place after a tumultuous period in the life of our small, almost unnoticeable planet and whilst he has written a billion words to try and relay his emotions on the subject of world peace, he has only spoken about forty words since 1999. If he was made king for a day, he would take the day off and go for a walk.

He also likes chocolate biscuits and milk.

And dogs.

Space

Voids between galaxies are known as interstellar space. Oddly within this space, nothing can survive. Its density of material particles is almost immeasurable and the heat in these vacuums makes it rarefied and dangerous; so dangerous in fact that scientists believe it would be folly to send the most robust and minuscule probe fearful for its existence. It is also very difficult to measure the size of interstellar space because its wobbles like the knees of a drunken man walking home on a tightrope

Complex plasma, which possesses a cosmic filamentary structure, is denser than the universe and its existence itself continues to bamboozle and confuse the world's greatest thinkers and astronomers. Astrologers as well, but lots of things confuse them. Impassable dust moves at billions of miles per hour, meaning travel through these spaces is not feasible and its intricate existence would destroy all meaningful structures. It is the final frontier that will never be seen to all intents and purposes. It houses nothing. Zero. Nought. Zip. Nowt. Except for Bellsurp.

Deep Space

All known, visible planets flow around their own gravitational pull and each one exists in its own part of space as part of a microcosm in relation to the vast plains of emptiness, but Bellsurp is somehow different. For reasons nobody can explain, Bellsurp is a shape-shifting giant (sometimes quite small) of a planet that moves in straight lines but follows non-standard lines of space as though the lines themselves don't exist. It doesn't conform to any science principles and nobody can explain why its people cannot only escape its flexible borders as they head off into the never-ending darkness of space to explore but even more confusing to the thinkers amongst them is how they ever find their way home.

It is round, sometimes, but as often as not, it is straight, sort of, and from a distance, it is green, perhaps, although its primary colour scale is not what you could use to define the different shades it produces. Colours regularly mingle and stray into one another, creating patterns that are regularly pleasing, occasionally ugly and periodically terrifying.

Inhabitants

Time also shakes and whirrs a bit too much for standard science on Bellsurp and organising meetings tends to create chaos by simply trying to get more than one Bellsurpian to the same spot within days of another. The term 'any other business' can mean anything from 'speak up' to 'let's never discuss this, or anything like it ever again' and meetings are often called to ensure that certain matters are never debated. The population figures range anywhere from millions to confusion and as counting tends to be the job of certain individuals, it never causes an issue unless enough sweeties don't turn up. That eventuality is rare.

Science

Amongst the inexplicable intricacies of Bellsurpians is their ability to listen to, convert and understand languages from planets all around the galaxies that surround them and many of them listen intently to entertainers from the era of Laurel and Hardy to the comedy stylings of Mrowaartt and NNcroo from Tringaipando in the Rapngt Sector. If nothing else, the Bellsurpians love a good laugh.

Culture

Nature doesn't compute within the confusing parameters either, but the *principle* of nature sometimes does. Bellsurpians seem to be able to love and hate without knowing or understanding why and although they are, by and large, frightened of anything they can't explain, and most of what they can, they possess a well-trained and well-supported armed services programme.

Protection

The groupings fall vaguely into factions of fliers, walkers and swimmers, as well as the much-vaunted hoppers, who many believe to be supernatural beings as staying upright on two feet is an onerous enough task for many without the threat of removing a limb from the ground for ambulation, regardless of duration. In addition to the admirable service folk, Bellsurp also houses Calistones. A breed apart due to their ability to read minds, float, and produce high-quality treacle, a skill that passed into folklore and was often questioned on the basis that no other Bellsurpian had actually witnessed the treacle manufacture or taste. Calistones may have fibbed about their sugary construction skills

Competition

Military intelligence was questionable. Sporadically, at meetings of the military clusters, complicated plans are put forward by the military thinkers, who would be immediately put down by the *real* Bellsurpian thinkers who were always around to ensure the military thinkers could find their way to and from the meetings. Sinister rumblings, however, had been rising from the masses as the flier's leaders looked to take over the running of the planet from the clever people. The almost clever King was aware of the rumblings through and made sure the clever people kept him apprised of any such grumbles, which accounted for a mainly happy and peaceful existence in their own bit of quasi-space that would never be found and therefore never be in danger from outsiders.

Life and Royalty

As Kings went, this King was pleasant enough, but what he definitely was not was a really clever person and as such could be convinced by certain aspects of fear that would make his copper crown rattle on his tall, bony head

"We just need to make sure the King is aware that one planet, in particular, is potentially a danger to Bellsurp," General Battleprop said as he addressed his peers during a meeting that inadvertently managed to get everyone together at the same time.

"Says who?" asked a clever person, cleverly.

"We've been listening," answered the belligerent General without hesitation. "These people are constantly being fooled by screen personalities who can convince them to do implausible and unthinkable things. Who's to say they couldn't convince them to invade Bellsurp?"

After a very brief tête-à-tête, the response was concise. "Because they are too stupid."

"Stupid like a Garoontah," said the general and gained a little more credence amongst his fans, who all knew Garoontahs were the most cunning of all of the Oontah family. What had started some considerable time before would continue as a spat between the seemingly violent men of war and the polar opposite clever people, even though the shape of Bellsurp didn't allow poles to be opposite. In a continuous clash for support and succour, the argument would rage on and as long as the case could always be quashed, then the King was content that no intergalactic squabble would occur on his watch and as Bellsurpians lived for thousands of years, it was a considerable watch.

Ambition

Battleprop, however, knew if he persisted, one of his attempts would get through the defence mechanism of the planet's cleverest scientists and the sooner that happened, the sooner he would gain the confidence of the King in making him the most important man ever to lead the Royal commander by his Royal nose, which was a very substantial hooter.

The clever people, however, were confident he would never get past their impenetrable line of well-thought-out, reasoned logic and knew that invading another planet so far away that just finding it would create enough fear to put the fliers off. Furthermore, they also knew that military intelligence equated to the Paranoontah, the daftest of the Oontah family.

Confidence of that level could only spell disaster, though and as sure as night follows a different night, then part of the afternoon, then back to mid-morning depending on which way the suns were catching the horizon, it happened. Without knowing how it transpired, the military men managed to convince the King to allow them to send a mission to a planet so far away that they may never return. They also managed to get the clever people to agree to it.

Further to that, they managed to convince all parties that unless the mission commander could irrefutably prove that the inhabitants of the far-off place were thoughtful, caring and non-threatening to the rest of the known and unknown space world, they would be educated or destroyed.

Cynical scientists sat in silence as the mission started and silently mulled over their own shortcomings while Battleprop sensed his own upsurge in power. As his subordinates took off to ask a few questions of the distant residents, he mused about snatching power by giving the go-ahead to blow Earth to pieces

Best Laid Plans

With all that had happened, the mission commander decided he could never have predicted a relationship with an older man, albeit a relationship borne out of symbiosis and focusing mainly on getting the stubborn old goat to buy something.

Some time ago, it seemed that this strategy was just about as straightforward as it could possibly be.

Some time ago, though, he had never met a human.

Little did he know, the human he did engage would turn out to be a cantankerous old goat who crawled out of bed each day with one intention; to wind up as many people as he could.

What he could never have known was with a whole planet to choose from, he would decide on an island so small and secluded that if Mrs Deighton sneezed at number 16 Sea Crescent, Mrs Cambrian at number 1 Hill View would say, "Bless you."

It would have been impossible to even consider that after a trip as long as the one they had taken at light speed, his choice to stop here would cause the kind of confusion that it did simply by applying basic science.

And it would have completely befuddled him to contemplate that his own basic knowledge of his planet's science was so far advanced on this world that his mere presence would create so much apathy imparted by the local's refusal to accept he existed

Most of what transpired would have been too far-fetched to believe if it had been foretold.

But it did

Meet The Gang If You Must

It was two in the morning when it first happened, but as it was two in the morning, everyone was asleep and missed it.

It had been a Tuesday morning and today was also a Tuesday morning, but because it was eight hours later, some people were around to witness it. However, if people don't want to buy what you sell, it's a waste of time and energy trying to convince them to buy what you sell. In fact, it wasn't until they climbed onto their craft and left that the few people present took any notice. When the few people in the vast gardens of Sunny Dew Asylum that saw them leave made the relevant information available to their carers, they weren't believed. It was proving difficult.

It was an important decision, so everyone turned up at the meeting and agreed that a change of venue could be a good idea, but unfortunately, it was deemed appropriate to reconstitute the two in the morning time, so consequently, another attempt failed.

The next visit was a huge success with twenty very small people gathering around, accompanied by three larger people and although they couldn't hold their attention for long, everyone agreed this was the best time and venue. To formally promote the agreement, another foray was arranged for the same time and venue the next day, where the same group of small people and the three big ones were present.

"Show them what we've got, sir." Delius urged Captain Swamsoot, using the language decipherer that enabled them to come to Earth with confidence.

"Certainly," answered mission commander Captain Swamsoot with the same effusive showmanship demonstrated in a carnival. "Come and look at this, you pack of scabby half-wits," he shouted to gain their attention and confidence. "You wouldn't believe the problems this little beauty is going to sort out for you, you spineless little prats." Incredibly, the audience seemed caught up in the spin like a cow in a tornado. "You'll never find anything like this in your stupid high street outlets where people like you still shop, not knowing anything better. No stupid fools like you bunch of morons have witnessed anything quite like it, so come along and see what we've got for you." And the small crowd slid comfortably towards Captain Swamsoot the way rats move towards soggy bread.

Above their heads, the Sun shone warmly down, producing a sense of well-being that made the sale easier, but still, the captain needed more of a push and thrust to completely captivate his audience. "As you're all so positively docile, I'm willing to throw in a couple of pieces of paper for nothing, but you'll have to ring this number, which will cost you an absolute fortune, you dimwits."

It certainly seemed to work and Swamsoot grinned like a man happy enough to spit a distance. As the travelling pack had come over twenty million gortanties, they were delighted to have gained such a level of success so quickly. Back on Bellslurp, where pessimists generally ruled the roost, their knockers made light of the trip and questioned the eligibility for the prize competition with the ominous twist.

Now, the breakthrough had happened, so Swamsoot jerked a thumb over his shoulder towards the craft where the technicians knew instinctively what to do.

As the good captain held captive his crowd of small people, technician number one sent the message via the intergalactic whiz-rod.

"Activity one is a success. Tiny people are gaping in awe. Clearly, tiny people are…" It was a piddling point, but technician number one decided to temporarily cut the message short until he could ascertain the full extent of the tiny people's station and status.

Slipping out of his Merodian chair, he skipped down the walkway and across the grassed area where Swamsoot was pointing aggressively at the tiny people and appealing to their sense of provocation.

"Each of you has the brains of a camel's bottom and couldn't..."

"Excuse me, sir." Technician number one interrupted. "I've started the message of gloatery but realised we don't have their position in the heraldry."

"What?" answered Swamsoot without animosity.

"I can't even tell the knockers how these tiny people inform their subjects of their decisions, sir."

Without any further continuation, Swamsoot ordered the party back on board the vessel and they went away for supper. He left behind a group of youngsters and three Brazilian teachers who had been told that their school, on the outskirts of Rio, would be visited by a travelling circus from Russia. As interested as they had been, they were all disappointed not being able to understand a word of what had been said. All things considered, though, if their craft hadn't looked so much like a helicopter, they might have caused a stir.

It was two full days before Swamsoot had been able to determine what status the tiny people enjoyed and as the translation of 'children' meant 'beasts of power' in

Bellsurpian, he returned to the venue, thrilled at the prospect of selling his wares to great beasts with enough power and stature to win him the prize.

There they were. The same children looked less than the expected beasts of power, but nonetheless, as the Bellsurpian dictionary had detailed, the children were terrifying monsters. More than one of the beasts wore pink clothes, a colour they had never seen before and presumed it carried a venomous poison and cautiously avoided touching them. Some years previously, a travelling party had landed on a planet where the inhabitants were large, ginger frog-like monsters who ate all of their clothes and called them names. Naturally, venomous poison was nowhere near as dangerous as garment theft or name-calling, but now safety was of paramount importance and the decision not to touch the 'pink ones' was swiftly passed down the line and adhered to. In time, the 'pink ones', or 'girls' as they came to be called, would become revered as the ultimate fighting beasts, as deemed by all Bellsurpians, who were the biggest, softest, nancy-like race in the whole of creation.

Just Pay Attention

Bellsurp was unlike most other planets in that it couldn't produce an army of any note to put up a face-to-face fight against the meekest of opposition. In fact, they could barely muster an argument without a number of the collective bursting into tears or running screaming from wherever the discussion took place. Often, the only reason they wouldn't run scared from a meeting room was down to the meetings being held at night, therefore meaning it was too dark outside for them to venture out alone. Bellsurpians were, in short, big softies.

For years, the Bellsurpian strategic committee had considered implementing a compulsory assertive behaviour class for all residents but, unfortunately didn't have the nerve to pass the resolution. Most of the afternoon chats were taken up with the fear of the imminent evening, dusk, and eventually darkness, which engendered a feeling of dread throughout the race.

"What are you doing at dusk?"

"I'm heading off to the wild caves to attack some of the dragons."

"Really? Can I come?"

"Of course, you can, as long as... Oh, I've just remembered I have to... I mean, it's the time of the year... Sorry I have to go now. My mum's called me in for my tea, and it's bath night."

Sadly, every community in Bellsurp encountered this type of nonsensical discussion every day. This type of turgid exchange led to Swamsoot's party of travellers finding their way to Earth.

Unlike the enormous majority of Bellsurp, Swamsoot had some fortitude, albeit only in comparison to his fellow Bellsurpians and nobody took up the challenge as quickly. Sitting in his garden one sunny, muggy afternoon, a call on his newly installed whiz-rod told him a proclamation was on the way, which included a potential prize never before seen on the planet. There might have been more potential players in the noble, well-advertised game, but Swamsoot and his crew stole a march on the whole of Bellsurp by agreeing to collect the information and read it on the way to the destination. In addition, the revered army generals had made it clear that the sideline to this expedition could well mean the end of the civilisation on the planet known as Earth and potentially any flight members who happened to be ensconced there at the time.

Swamsoot had overlooked that part. One of the technicians had questioned the rationale for taking off without understanding the full extent of the expectations, but a number of high-brow comments put him firmly in his place.

"Scared, are you?

"Oh, who's a big baby then?"

"Shut your gob," and so on and so forth, thus denying him the opportunity to understand the error of his ways and the potential mutiny was ended just after take off. Swamsoot was confident as he initially tried to explain the theory behind the journey and only when he realised his ignorance did he panic. Confidence slipped away like the last blob of toothpaste down the sink as he stood up to address his loyal crew, knowing he couldn't let them know the bits that he knew. The scary bits.

"Comrades," he shouted, practising his Earth language, as they all listened through the automatic translating earphones. "Today, we go to… It isn't important where we go because we go… with enormous… things… and stuff."

A thunderous ovation followed a moment's silence, and Swamsoot marched proudly back to his room to scratch his head and wonder at the ineptitude of his fellow countrymen, women and Calistones. A very high percentage of his crew were Calistones, which made control easier than dealing with the more belligerent of the Bellsurpian masses, although the Calistones were, generally speaking, dim. Swamsoot was deep in thought when the list of crew members was passed to him an hour after take-off.

"Thank you, Ditty," he said kindly to the uninformed sergeant who arrived with the personnel list. "Is this everyone we have on board?"

"No, sir," Ditty answered candidly. "We've been unable to formally count the stowaways as they haven't shown themselves yet."

"But we know how many of them there are?"

"Yes, sir."

"Good," Swamsoot crowed pensively. "Very good. There appears to be a large number of Calistones here, Ditty. We haven't encouraged more than the necessary quota, have we?"

"No, sir. The numbers have been totted up and we hit the regional recommendations to point zero-two. We did consider bringing another couple, but that might have meant more paperwork, sir."

"Well done, Ditty. We can't have more bureaucracy than is needed on a trip like this."

"Oh no, sir," Ditty interrupted. "I meant toilet paper. The Calistones are renowned for overuse of the facilities and the paper…"

Swamsoot raised his hand casually. "I understand, Ditty. Well done. Can you bring me the rota sheets for the kitchen and two bags of whatever delicacies we brought from the Landbark Gunk Emporium?"

"Certainly, sir. I see your sweet tooth is aroused," Ditty noted observantly.

"Yes, it must have been aroused by the literature in this shiny magazine here with the Bare Bellsurp Babes. They certainly know how to make a man froth at the mouth."

"Finest cooks on Bellsurp, sir." And the two men tipped back their heads to momentarily contemplate what they had left behind in the form of good food and nice teeth. Bellsurpians had the whitest, shiniest, straightest teeth in the Galaxy and the only people to dispute this were the Wellbirdians and legend had it;; they were produced from the genes of the envy plant. Ensuring the teeth stayed perfect was down to the Bare Bellsurp Babes, who made puddings for all of the major chains on Bellsurp, including the Landbark Gunk Emporium.

Many of the competitors to the LGE were viewed as second best to the products of this particular store, as they employed more Babes in the Heffner kitchen than most and consequently attracted queues as well as investment. It was a lot to leave behind.

"Right then, Ditty," Swamsoot spluttered, disengaging himself from the daydream that they had joined in. It was a mysterious trait of Bellsurp to be able to share a daydream and frequently resulted in pairs of strangers missing their stops on the bus. "Let's get back to work and see what we have in the galley."

"Yes, sir," Ditty responded, climbing out of the trance as though inebriated. "I'll get on it right away and bring you a wafer-thin stowaway as well." Swamsoot watched him walk away and worried for Bellsurpians, who might someday have to depend on soldiers like Ditty.

Being unable to hold reasonable conversations with his team unsettled Swamsoot to the extent that he rarely contemplated such an ill-thought-out manoeuvre unless circumstances dictated and following the original excursions to Rio some considerable time after the mission commenced, the situation now warranted such a dialogue.

Swamsoot spoke loudly and assertively over the sound system on the craft. "This is your captain speaking. If you aren't doing anything else, can you all come to the meeting auditorium as opposed next to the Mover's Hall, please?"

Knowing how aggressive he could be, everyone turned up without exception, apart from three Calistones who were busy on the toilet. Milling around in the huge room, many people would have been intimidated by such an address, but he strode meaningfully through the throng to take up his place at the platform to the front of the room.

"Hello there," he said softly and stood back, allowing the thunderous applause to subside. "It's about the trip we just had. It appears we didn't have as much information as we thought we had and we didn't find out the pecking order of the creatures." Although he expected it, the second round of applause agitated him slightly. "Please, There's no need to applaud everything I say in this particular address." All things considered, he wished he hadn't bothered, as the third round of applause peeved him further. Sometime later, however, the applause had subsided sufficiently to allow him to make an address without punctuation, thus denying further opportunity for interruption. "The thing is, we were supposed to get enough information to figure out not only who they are and why they behave the way they do, but why they allow people to do what they do, as well as who is in charge and why they are in charge, the food they eat, their preferences, their favourite colours, their favourite food, the best Massimals and whether or not they have any tendencies towards other groups, namely us, that might prove problematic." A brief pause to take a breath and a further attack before the applause took off. "Additionally, we need the average size, the average weight, the average number of statistics they take every week, the average…" Swamsoot looked carefully at his audience, who had noticeably switched off at the second mention of the word average. Momentarily, he considered progressing with the list to get it out of the way but decided instead to say no more than was necessary to give them enough but not too much to deal with. "We need to go back, to a different place perhaps and find out who's in charge," he said and padded away from the stage before the clapping became unbearably loud. Years of experience told him the ovation would carry on for at least half of the night and only the brightest of the crew would realise there was to be no encore. Had he stayed any longer, he may have been forced to endure an evening of tributes as often arranged at short notice for all great Bellsurpians, but he took the judicious route and hid back in his room until morning.

A bright light shone through his window in the morning, which surprised him greatly, namely due to his room having no windows. Climbing off his bed, he scratched his head and wondered why this mysterious situation had come about whilst he slept. Swamsoot was a thinker and his family had been renowned as the 'thinking Bellsurpian's thinking family' back on Bellsurp, but this had him, temporarily at least, mystified. Pulling on his trousers, he decided to get straight to the bottom of this puzzle.

"What's this hole in my room for?" he shouted down his microphone with vigour and authority. On the other end of the communication line, he could hear scurrying as though one hundred- and one-blind mice had just heard a whoop of farmer's wives opening their cutlery drawers.

As was often the case under such testing circumstances, nobody would answer the question. Amongst their many skills, the Calistones were able to detect anger in the tone of a voice and quickly relayed that fear to their fleeing colleagues. They, in return, had run to hide under anything that would lift, including those who had overslept. It was one of the most endearing points about the Bellsurpians that they were coy enough to hide rather than face confrontation but silly enough to believe they could not be detected if they were warm and cozy.

In a fearsome rage, Swamsoot marched out of his room and into the long, winding corridor that led its way through a myriad of honeycombs and dwints where all manner of travellers could, and frequently did, hide.

During the sleeping hours, he would often walk these areas like a vanguard for all that was Bellsurpian, whistling as he went to let his crew know he was up and about and that they were safe to sleep with him on duty. That he was keeping them awake with the inane whistling and was often drunk and sleepwalking meant nothing. Now, however, he was filled with rage and another emotion that he wasn't sure about, but felt confident it would come to him eventually. At the far end of the corridor, as many as ten Calistones were dozing on the floor and didn't so much as raise an eyelid to make a note of the angry skipper, although they all picked up the emotion and dreamt about it as he passed by.

For years, Swamsoot had raged with relative indifference, but shortly before the trip, he spent some time with an anger management consultant who taught him to manage his anger to perfection. "Money well spent," he deduced as he felt the heat of his blood reach the purple face temperature and still his anger grew uglier. By the time he found the offending individual, his face could be the colour of a dragon's nostril if he maintained this rage. Just then, more or less when he expected it, the rage subsided as he realised he no longer cared about who put the hole in his wall, or at least not to the degree of face bursting shades of scarlet. Now that he was in the vicinity, however, he decided to ask about the introduction anyway and within a moment, the Calistones picked up on pleasantish vibes and woke everyone up.

"Morning men, erm... etc," he said in the same pleasantish fashion. "How's everyone feeling today then?" A general mutter sprouted from the silence before one brave voice came to the fore.

"Everyone here, or everyone everywhere, sir?"

Not for the first time, Swamsoot was a little taken aback by the reasonableness of the literal question. Although he had lived amongst Calistones all of his life, their grasp of reality confused him to the degree of somewhere between exasperation and fury. Right now, he had bottomed out at about dumbfounded.

"It's not important. It's really more of a salutation in essence." Sadly, it was early in the day and he wasn't thinking to his full capacity, but he had said it and there was no point in retracting the statement as any attempt to do so would only further the confused plight. Amidst the next round of mumbles, a squawk could be heard clearing its throat.

"Sir," asked Elderberry Gladly, a midget Calistone from the dark sector of Bellsurp. "We once steeped some peas in the essence of parrot juice and sold it for embalming fluid.

Is a salutation, in essence, any more legal than that? I only ask because four of my cousins are still locked up."

"Well, Gladly," Swamsoot started. "There is more than one type of essence, of that there is no doubt, but..." And there he decided he couldn't be bothered to carry on with this line of nonsense.

"Attention!" he shouted with some ferocity and left the room as they scrambled into lines of disquiet and rabble. Having captained Bellsurpian crafts for many years, it seemed this pleonastic behaviour would continue, so he decided upon prudence and left them alone.

Beyond the solar system in which they now roamed, Swamsoot had left home and a family. Fair enough, he didn't much care for them either, but they were his and if he wanted to miss them, it would be his prerogative. From time to time, mainly on occasions such as this, he missed the home and family he didn't much care for. Calistones had their place on his ship, but only if he could avoid them. A number of odd happenings had occurred recently, but he couldn't be bothered to get to the bottom of them, so wandered aimlessly for an unspecified time before stopping at one of the ship's hailers to punch in his password and submit a direct instruction to all on board within his charge.

"Just for today," his voice boomed over the craft's PA system. "We will do no exploratory work. In fact, everyone will go to bed again and remain there until tomorrow morning. Goodnight."

Reared With Social Graces

On a small island North of Scotland, a late-middle-aged man was walking to the paper shop with his dog. It was a beautiful spring morning and the sky was as blue as a small boy's legs when he's playing football in January. Not many of the locals bothered to look up at the sky on the island of Scroat, but just for today, Tam Wilson decided to stare at the blue yonder in awe.

Oddly, it didn't fill him with awe or anything close to veneration, although he was slightly perplexed at the craft that looked a bit like a helicopter. Not too much like a helicopter, but enough for him to describe it as one should the need arise. Although it hovered a few hundred feet above him, Tam was sure he should have been able to hear the engines or at least the whirring of the blades that he couldn't quite see. "Must be going too quickly," Tam said quietly to himself before taking out his hip flask and taking a hefty slug of whisky. "Come on, Jack," he ushered his dog. "Let's go to the pub." And hundreds of feet above him, a silent crew of many considered this place an option to land and a potential reason to wake up their captain. By way of their technology, every word he had said to Jack, the dog, was overheard and translated through the whiz-rod.

"So did the little hairy fellow say anything back to him?" seemed a reasonable question.

"Sssshhhh!" was the communal answer. As decent a man as he was, the whole crew was aware that waking up Swamsoot on a day's sleeping assignment could be serious trouble for the wake-upee. Naturally, the Calistones had read his mind and were aware he was occasionally giggling as Oliver Hardy kicked Stan Laurel up the rear end. Strange dreams indeed, they thought.

Swamsoot enjoyed spending time alone on the long, laborious trips across space, although he was more excited about this one than any other he had marshalled. He was more excited because he was aware of what Earth had to offer by way of entertainment and boorish newspaper stories. Inside his room, he dredged through mountains of data, accrued by the medium of danatronical starflash, the Bellsurpian equivalent of the intergalactic internet. Amidst the mountains of information lay the pictures he loved the most and every time he looked at them, the Calistones were aroused by his thoughts. Being innocent of any carnal thoughts, the Calistones were bemused by the feelings they experienced and although they were too conservative to discuss it, they all felt the same guilt. During the early years, Swamsoot had yearned to travel to places far away and although his Father had bullied him into the flight corps, he never expected to fulfil his dreams at such an early age. Unlike most of his professional peers, Swamsoot was roughly one hundred and six years old, some eighty or so years younger than the average space captain and almost two hundred years younger than the first Bellsurpian to fly a craft filled with such an unreserved crew of lunatics. Damalgo Winstonian Swamsoot was a very proud Bellsurpian.

Paid To Make Tough Decisions

Scroat was a quiet island off mainland Britain and was ferociously Scottish by definition. Many of the residents were boastfully patriotic about their heritage and positively jingoistic about the fact that nobody other than Scroats had ever settled there. The local public house was adorned with paintings of ancient Scroats who had fought off menace after menace to preserve this preserve in a place where only the most weather-beaten, tough, allegiant characters could survive only the dourest individuals ever tried. Alex McWilliamatic hung over the fireplace with a ferocious-looking team at his heels and the Scroats felt obliged to raise their hats or tug their forelocks as they passed by in a sign of respect for the first man to have eaten raw horse on the island. Horses now formed a fundamental part of the islander's diet and only since they ran out of horses had someone suggested they have sausage delivered from the mainland. It wasn't as good as a horse, but it was edible.

Tam Wilson bundled his way into the pub with Jack bringing up the rear, and trundled to the bar.

"Morning," he delivered his usual terse growl without checking to see who he was addressing. "Are we open yet?" Being demonstrably linked to Scotland, the bar was open.

"Yes, Tam," answered Millie Corwilly. "Of course we're open. A pint?" she asked with more than a hint of sarcasm and being as coy himself as a maidenly virgin from the land of no kisses, Tam delayed his answer whilst he rubbed his chin with pensive contemplation.

"A pint, eh?" he mused, but before his muse was complete, Millie had poured and served the pint of heavy. It was the way with Scroat that no cash passed hands until the last day of every month and Millie chalked another of many marks onto a board behind the bar to record Tam's debt, ever plummeting into a beer mire. "Is this the finest beer you have?" enquired the Scottish sot with just a hint of respect for the barmaid.

"Just drink it," she replied with just a hint of rudeness. Outside, the clouds passed overhead with a light breeze behind them and the day seemed as perfect as ever in this rural haven that the Scroats held so dear. Tam Wilson took a long slug out of his glass and spoke without directing his stare at anyone in particular.

"Did you see the helicopter?" However, as he didn't appear to be speaking specifically to anyone, nobody answered. The question went unheeded and the reply was never actively pursued.

Meanwhile, many feet above them, a helicopter-shaped craft hovered silently whilst its crew prepared to land, although their inability to *remain* silent would infuriate their captain before too long. On the door to Swamsoot's cabin hung a message that terrified every space travelling Bellsurpian to the extent that their faces would contort like a child's when seeing the dentist's drill for the first time. It read;

'Don't wake mc up, or I will be furious'. Anyone who dared to wake him up would be in trouble. Big trouble!

Inevitably, someone woke him up and he simply tutted with a sanctimonious air and carried on with his business, reasonably happy that he had at least spent a few hours relaxing in his room. As was the case under such circumstances, he demanded a roll call and bought himself another hour of peace and quiet whilst all of the crew panicked their way into formation. Quiet and dejected, his walk to the assembly point was almost slovenly as he meandered down the main walk to the area designated as the reception. Ahead of him, beyond the door to the congregation spot, he could hear them all flustered and abashed with the confusion that set in whenever they were asked to stand in a straight line. Swamsoot smiled coyly as he entered the room to a mixture of groans and jubilance, seriously considering wasting a pithy comment on them. He declined.

"Team!" he shouted before realising he had nothing to say to them. "Are you ready?"

"Yes," they shouted in response.

"What are you ready for?" he chanced his arm. Naturally, this was a far trickier dictum for the assembled mass, and as suspected, they all mumbled, blushed, or simply fell over. Bellsurpians were renowned in their universe for not being able to deal with fastidiousness. Although they were excellent at dealing with pest problems, a simple question often brought out the worst in them. As the seconds rolled into minutes, Swamsoot realised his charges were a collection of ignoramuses, although some of them had faults as well. Some of them remained prostrate on the floor whilst the remainder still in the upright position began running into one another as though stricken with contagious blindness. Like a proud Father, he called them to order by taking the immediate pressure off.

"I'm going to the toilet. I expect you to be prepared when I return." As he walked out of the room, though, he thought carefully about how the panic would set in, as he hadn't suggested a time scale for his return. Meanwhile, way below them, an argument had started.

"It doesn't say you have to shake them anyway," Millie Corwilly shouted at Tam, who had broken into pedantic mode.

"Yes, it does," Tam replied without raising his voice. "It clearly says, 'shake before opening'."

"Well, yes, I know it says that, but that doesn't mean you have to do it, does it? It's only a suggestion."

"No, it isn't. It's a fairly clear instruction. 'Shake before opening'. Why would they put it on the pack if you aren't supposed to do it?"

"Well, if you're that bothered about it, just shake them." Millie was usually very cool when it came to dealing with Tam, but sometimes... "They won't taste any different whether you shake them or not."

Tam lifted his head from reading the 'clear' instructions. "You're missing the point here, Millie. When I purchase a packet of nuts, I purchase the finished article, not an unshaken product. I demand service and respect, becoming someone of my standing in this community."

"Tam Wilson," Millie started like a Mother about to badger the life out of a drunken husband in front of her children. "If you were afforded the respect you deserve in this community, you'd be picking the seaweed off the beach and selling it for beer tokens." Across the bar, the locals kept their heads buried in newspapers and each other's conversations to avoid being dragged into the mire.

"My dear lady," Tam hooted with derision. "I'll have you know, whether you care to accept it or not, the Wilsons were the first family on this island, so by definition, I am the island elder and, therefore, the single most influential person in the whole of this municipality."

Amidst the nonsense in the clouds overhead, the phrase was picked out as being 'vitally important,' and Swamsoot was immediately informed, whereupon he rushed, as much as a meandering man could rush, to the communications port. Two of his most trusted whiz-rod mechanics were almost delirious with excitement when he entered their domain to see them knocking each other sideways in childlike play, normally associated with primary school nitwits.

"Sir," hollered Batmask. "We appear to have found a leader".

"Oh yeah," Batmorsk questioned with puerile sincerity. "So 'we' appear to have found a leader, do we?"

"I think that's what I said." Batmask retorted just as childishly but with just a hint more venom. "In fact, I *know* that's what I said. Idiot."

"Oh, I'm an idiot, am I?"

"No, you're actually a great big idiot."

Swamsoot hung his head like a puppy just found looking over its latest deposit on a new carpet.

"Boys! As much as I commend the way you've been swatting up on Earth's politicians, I think you can wait until we're amongst them before behaving like them. Do I make myself clear?" Both men nodded, although his common-sense approach did nothing more than confuse them. "So, who have you found that appears to be a leader?" he asked, suddenly with an effusive childlike quality of his own.

"It's a man, well, a human man, with a small hairy partner and what appears to be an insatiable thirst, sir." From his experience, he knew they'd be right, mainly because Batmask and Batmorsk were always right. Although Bellsurp didn't actually have bores, Batmask and Batmorsk were the nearest things to it. Most nights, they would stay awake to watch each other fall asleep to monitor sleep patterns and report on it the moment the lucky one woke up. In addition to this quality lifestyle, Batmask and Batmorsk were identical in every way and only enjoyed each other's company. Swamsoot hated them both but loved having them around as he trusted them with his life.

Having spent their formative years on a mountain, Batmask and Batmorsk, or Batty and Batty, as they liked to be called, knew how to cook a meal from a spoonful of spit and a handful of dirty grass. That it looked and tasted like grass and spit was an irrelevance, although an irrelevance on Earth was a positive enigma on Bellsurp. Batty and Batty were genuine contenders for enforced volunteers in biology lesson dissections.

Nonetheless, their ability to identify a flea part from nine miles made their input to voyages like this essential and Swamsoot wouldn't have left home without them. The travel across space was made for insignificant input and these two boys offered that in abundance. In truth, they made a reputation for themselves by being the first Bellsurpians to formally repel aggressive interplanetary coalitions by telling their life stories, but for now, at least, they were an integral part of Swamsoot's team.

"So, do we know the name of this human man with the small hairy partner?" Swamsoot asked of his dull charges.

"We think he's called 'you old goat', sir. We will confirm that, of course, but apart from Tam, we haven't heard any other reference, sir."

"Excellent. Let's get a scene of 'you old goat' on the Whiz-rod screen and see what we have to deal with."

"Certainly, sir," both Battys shouted in unison, as though trying to impress the people on the island of Wolfistar, back in the space bar sector 42. Volume played a big part in many Bellsurpian's lives, a principle lost on the Calistones who simply shouted telepathically.

Within a few seconds, a picture of Tam Wilson began to form on the Whiz-rod and soon presented itself clearly and concisely.

"All officers to the communications port," Swamsoot ordered over the PA system, stirring more confused circles turning by those still reeling from his last information exposition some thirty minutes beforehand. Knowing it would take some time and head battering, he decided to make some careful notes about 'you old goat' and his little hairy partner.

Tam Wilson looked fairly normal, by Earth standards at least, although his little hairy partner was a cause for concern. He viewed Tam carefully as he wobbled lightly on his feet from his position at the bar to a small, round table some ten feet away. There, he unhappily shook a small plastic bag and began to rip open the corner while staring menacingly at the woman behind the bar.

"That wasn't too difficult for you, was it, you old goat?" she enquired of him sincerely. Swamsoot made notes.

"Perhaps you should have taught him how to do that years ago, Jack." Jack simply wagged his tail.

"Hmm," Swamsoot muttered to himself. "The dangerous silent type. Batty, get everyone fell in." Batmask immediately jumped to his feet and would have left the room earlier had he not waited to haughtily grin at Batmorsk for being the captain's choice. With an ostentatious show of whiz-rod skills, Swamsoot focussed in on Jack and his partner Tam Wilson, whose red nose and baggy eyes did nothing to disguise his alcohol intake. Batmorsk stared in wonderment as his master took careful note of everything that happened in the local pub. Meanwhile, his best friend and greatest enemy, Batmask, was falling everyone into line, not knowing that they were already in a state of severe confusion from the last order and still awaited the return of their boss. Trying to restore order to this mob was as easy as teaching two donkeys to tango on a telegraph wire, but he persisted until Swamsoot arrived and gave the command to prepare to land. With a nonchalant flick of the wrist and a camp wave of the hand, he spoke with interminable authority about going to meet two seemingly very sociable creatures.

"We're going in. And this time, it's personable!"

But They're My Idiots

Only a man like Tam Wilson could have delivered the type of insult to offend, although the harmless insult would have made a ten-year-old schoolboy cringe with an embarrassed droop of the shoulders. For as long as anyone could remember, Tam had been a rude man with an opinion of himself higher than a giant's balaclava, but tell him as they may, the locals could not stop his old discourteous ways.

"The thing is Jack," he informed his small dog, who sat with his ears folded over his head as though waiting for a childish chagrin. "The fat lady probably won't open the nuts in case she feels the urge to eat them. Fatty, fat, fat!"

True to his antecedence, the odd retort to the refusal to uncover his nuts was indeed petrifying and embarrassing. Millie turned her nose up the way she always turned up her nose at things to which she felt no fondness. On other occasions, Millie Corwilly had been known to turn her nose up at rats and snakes on the television and the picture of the island as painted by Martin Stedshaw. In fairness, the painting didn't displease her as much as Martin Stedshaw, but he left the island over ten years ago and the painting was all she had left to remind her of him. Thus, each time she looked at the framed likeness of her beloved homeland, she turned up her quaint nose in a sign of non-fondness.

If this type of behaviour had been unusual in Scroat, people in the vicinity would have taken more notice, but nobody cared as it was a virtual daily slice of the action. Sadly though, it was about as exciting as life ever became on Scroat, where the sheep didn't 'baa' because they were too bored. Cows didn't give milk because they couldn't be bothered and horses never messed in the streets because they wanted to give themselves a cleaning up job when they got home. In short, Scroat was as dull a place as anyone could ever dream about being stranded and after a million miles of space travel, it was about to be visited by Bellsurpia's finest crusaders, who were so excited, they could hardly contain the need to wee.

"Sir!" shouted a voice from the rear of the assembly point. "I need to have a wee."

"Alright," Swamsoot answered with the calmness of a seasoned ambassador. "Go and have a wee."

"Sir," shouted another anonymous voice. "Can I go too?"

"Yes, but make sure…"

Sir, can I go too, please?"

"And me?"

"What about me?"

"Me too?"

"Well, I want to go as well and…"

"Hold it," hollered the skipper, patience seeping from him like dribble from a sleeping baby's mouth. "Hands up, anyone who needs to go to the toilet for a wee?" Every visible palm could be seen within a second, but before he could speak, another question came at him out of the crowd.

"Is it only wee you're interested in, sir because I could do with a…"

"Right," Swamsoot interrupted swiftly. "Anyone who wishes to go to the toilet for whatever reason, please go now and try and get back without any fuss and as quickly as possible." Moments later, he stood alone in the hall and listened to moans and groans of relief and pleasure, followed by the craft's disposal units firing up. One by one, they sifted back in through the three sets of doors and began taking up their places, or at least as near as they could remember their places to be. All of them looked happier than when they had left, and none displayed any major nerves. The Calistones scanned the room to see if anyone was hiding any nervous disposition in relation to what would be waiting for them, but even they came back with no negative thoughts. In short, they were ready.

"Right then," started the captain once more. "We appear to have identified a member of the higher echelons of Earth and it looks like a human man with a small hairy partner. What we have been unable to establish is which of them holds the highest rank. That, however, doesn't matter too much, as we will be looking to impress them both with our ability to mystify and…"

"Whatever else it is, we do sir," Batmask whispered helpfully.

"Thank you, Batmask. And whatever else it is we do," he repeated with gusto for the enthusiastic onlookers. One of his many attributes was to take a crowd by the scruff of the neck and by the medium of shouting, crank them up into a positive frenzy. They loved him. "In the event, the picture down there turns ugly, what do we do?"

"Call them names and run away," came the menacing reply from the whole assembly.

"And what do we do if they run after us?"

"Cry like babies," was the unanimous response and Swamsoot was duly filled with the type of pride normally reserved for proud hares looking down on hordes of leverets. Many of his team would have gladly given their all if asked, although many more of them would have slid quietly under the sheets if asked for anything more than the bare minimum.

With his skill for manipulating his team, though, Swamsoot was confident he could get everything he wanted.

"Right then. I want ten volunteers to come down with me in the landing party to collect all of the data that will make us heroes back on Bellsurp."

Naturally, the silence was deafening and six short hours later, straws had been drawn and ten volunteers were being forced onto the landing basket by gunpoint. It now seemed pointless trying to motivate them further as most of the ten were in floods of tears, but his experience had taught him that an arm around the shoulder often worked wonders. This he did but made a mental note to punch them all when the chance arose.

Say That Again; I Dare You

Tam Wilson sat pensively, eating his nuts one at a time, all the while goading Millie by chewing with his mouth open. Millie was too much of a wise owl, though, to fall for his goading and simply carried on cleaning glasses until they were too thin to hold water. Occasionally, she'd break a glass and carry on cleaning the shards until the manager of the pub shook the remains from her bloodied hand. Nonetheless, she convinced herself that Tam Wilson didn't get to her and that she could handle his deportment, albeit linked to the manners of a garlic-eating pig with no social graces to talk of.

Tam, however, was convinced that she could not handle his manner and continued to bait her the way he had for as many years as he could remember. Millie was not alone, in as much as Tam had a variety of islanders for whom he spared no niceties and most of them hoped and prayed he would fall from the narrow coastal path he took home each night from the pub. Tam, sadly for them, was as sure-footed as a mountain goat and twice as smelly. Without ever having discussed it with anyone, everyone who came into contact with him deduced the smell came with the territory of bachelorhood, as the whole world knew that bachelors smell because they have nobody telling them to wash. Tam stank like a silage pit.

All in all, a smelly, rude, inconsiderate monster of a man like Tam was the worst welcoming party anyone could hope for. On his way home that night, the landing basket was sat on the ground in front of him and Swamsoot climbed out to greet a now drunken Scottish islander.

"Greetings, you idiot," he opened with.

"You're clearly a bigger idiot than me, although you're much too small to be a big idiot, you scabby little dwarf."

Hmm, Swamsoot thought. *He's good.* "Allow me to demonstrate some of my wares," he carried on unabated. "You're such a fool, you'll almost certainly want to purchase what I've got here in my trousers." If nothing else, this got Tam's attention just as Swamsoot turned his attention to Jack. "As for you, scrawny little stinky-bottomed creep, I suspect you will want as much as possible when you see what I have, mainly because you're too thick to know better."

Jack replied honestly, "Woof."

"Check what that means on the whiz-rod," he requested of the landing party at his rear. "And see if urinating when talking is unique to this country. I notice the small hairy one is doing it quite a bit and if it's rude not to do it, I'll start immediately."

"Yes, sir," Batmask answered in reassuring tones. "Should I bring you a jug of water if it is common practise, sir?" Swamsoot looked at Jack, who was busy cocking his leg on a tree.

"Better make it two."

Tam stared at them, barely capable of standing as still as the waves clashing beneath them onto the beach. Being prepared to ape their hosts, they all began to sway from side to side in perfect imitation, compelling Tam to question them aggressively.

"Are you trying to make me look like a barmpot here? Because if you are, you should know I don't take kindly to folk taking a lend. Do y' ken?"

Jack barked and Swamsoot panicked.

"Stay right where you are, you pair of blithering nuggets and I'll be right back when I've got something more overpriced and useless for you." Turning back to his team, he beckoned them all for a huddle, which they duly obliged.

"Does anyone know what the hairy one keeps saying?"

"I think he said something about a barmpot, sir."

"No, that was the big one. I mean the little hairy one."

"I think he said arr-aarr-aarr a couple of times, sir. I'm not sure, but I think that means he's ready to buy."

"Excellent," pronounced Swamsoot gloriously. "Let's get out the celebration mat and sing like Christians." Not knowing what he meant, the team simply shuffled uncomfortably to allow him the space to carry on with the selling technique that had brought them this far across the galaxy.

"Well then, you gaggle of morons. I think you thought I was about to fall for your little trick there, but I'm a lot smarter than I look."

"I don't doubt that," Tam mentioned contemptuously.

"It's about time you stopped acting stupidly and realised you're in the presence of something far more clever than you will ever understand." With a shrug of the shoulders, Tam snorted with all of the social graces of a dwarf with a chip on his shoulder having been invented to a giant's convention.

"OK," he muttered and walked uneasily past the Bellsurpians to head home.

"Playing hard to get, eh?" Swamsoot said casually. "Don't think I'm about to fall for the 'I don't care routine'. You'll be walking back here for this pointless purchase before long because you're as dim as a bulb without electricity. I know your type… I happen to know… You'll be back… You'll be… Right then, men," he continued without a pause. "Back to the ship. I think that's been an excellent interplanetary interaction you all witnessed there."

Being of sound mind, he wasn't always given to making throw-away remarks, particularly as most of his crew didn't understand irony. Now, however, he wasn't sure if *he* even meant what he was saying, such was the confusion caused by the rude man and his small hairy friend. One thing was for sure, though, the man's demeanour was that of a royal personage and at last, they had made contact with someone with sufficient status and rank to make a decision based on what they had travelled all of these miles for.

When the landing party arrived back on the Mother ship, they were greeted with hordes of eager Bellsurpians, all of which looked at the party for a reaction, then, when none was forthcoming, at the Calistones who, realising they were in the spotlight, concentrated their telepathic minds on Swamsoot. Within seconds, the good vibes had infiltrated their collective thoughts and their smiles produced an enormous howl of approval from the crowd.

They were welcomed back as heroes and carried shoulder-high around the landing platform, although shoulder height meant bending the legs to stop the feet from dragging along the floor in some cases. Cheers and sporadic singing broke out in a frenzy of happiness never before seen this far from home in a species normally frightened to go to the toilet alone, never mind millions of miles away from domestic solace. In all of their humble opinions, they had made the type of contact that would make them all legends back on Bellsurp, where space travel was a genuine privilege, usually reserved for high-ranking officials or victims of press gangs.

Either way, they were all here to enjoy and revel in the moment and as far as they could deduce. Rather than actually ask what had happened, the Calistones picked up on Swamsoot's happy demeanour and deemed that to be good news, thus, the celebrations would go on unabated. The captain, meanwhile, listened on his headphones to old Marx Brothers tapes, thus not allowing his frustrations to come to the attention of the well-meaning but inquisitive Calistones. *Tomorrow,* he thought. *We'll go back down there and really give him what for.* Tomorrow, of course, Tam Wilson would wake up with a hangover and no recollection of this evening's events and Jack peacefully dreamt of chasing rabbits.

Nice to Be Not Absent

Some years ago, on a planet many gortanties away, a group of people had invented a theory that suggested the only way to seek real power and status was to see how the older, less advanced planets coped. For years, they searched the universe, sparing no effort in an attempt to find the best group to emulate.

The land of Balkswatch was one such possibility, although further investigations led them to believe they would be eaten by the local workmen if they landed on that planet without an invitation. All things considered, it was deemed inappropriate to head to Balkswatch until all workmen had been tyrannised into a vegetarian proletariat. Beyond that, not many options for space travel actually existed and many years were wasted by trying to find an opening to start simulating other civilisations in the hope of bettering themselves.

What they had was unique, if not a little odd. Most of the people of Bellsurp could speak, eat, read and fly and others could invent things by thinking about them. A group of them could read minds and some others could make themselves invisible at the drop of a hat. Dropping hats was also a Bellsurpian pastime. Ultimately, they were a collection of cowards with incredible powers that nobody could explain, nor did they try to. Had they tried to explain it, someone would have taken offence and begun crying, on the basis it was scary. What they could do, which even they didn't understand, was make sense of nonsense, particularly someone else's nonsense. A remarkable ability to see faults in others and make a sound argument for them, not only applauding them but for making them into even bigger faults.

At the science block in which the great brains of Bellsurp trained, the manner of discussion was always based on improving something, even if it meant improving mistakes to make them more obvious.

The place where they trained was a large oval-shaped building with no windows originally, but soon thereafter changed to contain more window space than solid walls. This, it was agreed, would make it lighter for those who were frightened of the dark, as well as making it easier to see what was going on outside, as another of their traits was their nosiness.

More than anything, Bellsurpians loved to know everyone else's business. Harbour masters couldn't spit into the sea without someone seeing them and starting a rumour about how a spit had started a small wave, which then became a bigger wave and in no time at all, the original spit had flooded three small villages. In short, Bellsurpians were old blather masters.

As a race, they loved to chatter inanely about each other's shortcomings or cackle like drunken witches over a hot pot of doohicky jam. Naturally, their old tradition for jam-making made this particular norm easier, but catching the doohickys was never straightforward.

"There's a doohi… Oh, it's gone."

From a purely visual standpoint, it would be difficult to separate Bellsurpians from anyone other than everyone else in the universe. This, essentially, was down to their appearance being completely different to anyone else in the universe. Swamsoot was probably as near to 'normal looking' as any Bellsurpian came, but his short, dark, leery appearance didn't quite match up to the standard galaxy countenance, although he did uniquely possess a pair of eyebrows. Thick, dark, bushy eyebrows set him apart from his peers, except for the small community who lived in the village of Bushy Forehead back home. On Earth, Swamsoot could comfortably pass for a human, although the rest of the crew were hard-pressed to match up, mainly down to their height, or lack of it in actuality. Tiny-ness was a quality that the whole race was ferociously proud of and each tiny

Bellsurpian that arrived via parturition was welcomed with minute arms waving low in the air, accompanied by blasts of both voluntary and involuntary flatulence. For no clear reason, bottom control was not high on the list of priorities on Bellsurp, much to the indignation of the visitors from the planet Largehooter who, complain as they might, could not talk the natives into social graces to include gas control. As the population was so small in stature, it made up for its shortcomings by continuously striving to make the loudest body noises anywhere in the galaxy. It was one of the things they viewed as a great success.

"Any boy refusing to break wind loudly and during quiet spells of lessons will be publicly tormented," was the national insignia nailed over every school entrance the length and breadth of Bellsurp, dimensions that changed hourly.

Adjacent to the sign was the very noticeable flag of Bellsurp, another must on every school wall and a reminder that all that is Bellsurpian is not necessarily normal. Pure Bellsurpians were always banging on about the need to educate the youth of the day by drowning them in tradition and old traditions such as the flags and the windy-pops notices had to be upheld. Pure Bellsurpians were genuine elders of all communities, some of them achieving ages up to the equivalent of many hundreds of years. Elders were the most respected members of the locale in which they dwelt and everyone they spoke to hated them. Thankfully, they spoke to very few people, thus restricting their enemies to a manageable number should a fight ever ensue. This was always paramount in the thinking on Bellsurp, mainly down to the genetic cowardice, but also linked to the ignorance of how to actually make a fist.

What they didn't know, as they made plans to revisit Tam Wilson, was that he had made something of a reputation for wanting to fight anyone who looked at him the wrong way. Given that most Bellsurpians eyes were as crossed as a rubber man's legs mid-somersault, this would undoubtedly cause friction. It was to become a hard lesson to learn.

Swamsoot gathered his officers for a briefing before they set out on the next sortie to this strange, cold land below where at least one of the locals was royalty.

"Right then. It appears we have two candidates to consider, but which is the king and which is the subordinate?" Alongside him stood an easel with a red cloak draped across it, creating apprehension in the officers to the levels of needing the toilet. They whispered to each other about what it could possibly be, all the while reasonably convinced it would be a present for them due to the good work they had carried out the previous night. After a lengthy oratory from the skipper, to which nobody listened, such was the level of excitement about the present, Swamsoot unveiled two photographs of Tam and Jack. The audible dismay shook him for a while, but he managed to contain his emotions and carried on with the meeting, now confident that what he had already said had been wasted. "I think the little hairy one is probably the king, because he maintains a silent dignity, although he does appear to wee a little too much. The large, smelly one is a little…"

"Shabby, sir?" one of the executives offered by way of joining in.

"No, I meant he's a little aggressive for a king."

"Sir," interrupted Colonel Beltedchops. "King Fasstlegs is very aggressive and he's as much a king as any king that I know."

"Fair point Beltedchops, but King Fasstlegs was brought up on board games and shouting competitions, so naturally, we expect him to be a bit more assertive in his demeanour."

"He ate my auntie, sir."

"That was just a rumour, Beltedchops and please don't say he ate your house as well because that was just the second rumour that started after they found your auntie."

Being a good Bellsurpian soldier, Beltedchops accepted defeat graciously and started crying. Swamsoot carried on relentlessly. "So if we accept that the small hairy one is the king, do we then believe that the large aggressive one is either a bodyguard or another lower-ranking royal?" Not knowing the answer, the group assumed he was telling them rather than asking, so they all agreed.

"Absolutely, sir."

"Well deduced, sir."

"Three cheers for the…"

"Do not give me three cheers," he arrested the conversation before it took off beyond control. Swamsoot's humanoid eyebrows took on a look of seriousness as he scoured the room for any semblance of intelligence, then, after realisation sank in, reverted to plan A. "We need to find out which of the two humans we encountered last night is the leader. Do you understand?" Each of them peered at the other's reaction before dropping their chins to their chests rather than lie to the captain. "Come on!" he implored them. "It isn't a trick question. All I'm asking is, which one is in charge?"

Thankfully, colonel Toestump was a Calistone and managed to determine a train of thought. "Can I suggest we have five minutes, sir, to try and establish a united answer?"

Swamsoot was shocked. His question had been much too easy to have to make allowances for conference breaks, but Toestump's response had almost measured a point on the articulate scale, thus tempting him into acquiescence.

"If I agree to a one-minute adjournment, will you promise to come up with an idea between you, or at least an agreement to go and look for the answer in some sort of ordered fashion?" A general nodding and shaking signalled the agreement he so feverishly sought. "Right then, adjournment for…" One minute would be quite pointless. "Ten minutes."

"Twenty?"

Twenty minutes isn't bad, he thought secretly enough so as not to alert the Calistones. "Twenty it is then, but not a second more." And off they went to huddle and discuss the way forward, although they did not have the slightest idea what they were meant to be doing.

Swamsoot was in a predicament in that his remit was to include his crew in every decision and, preferably, to the extent of empowerment in the extreme. His recordings would have to show that this expedition demonstrated his crew's ability to make decisions. Every time he thought about it, he shook with a morbid fear. To consider the notion of handing over more than the insignificant amount of responsibility he had maintained outside of his control made him shudder like a bulldog hitting a tree after trying to stop on a frozen lake.

Being as radical as it was, nurturing inexperienced travellers was second nature to Bellsurp, but being as insightful as he was, no way was Swamsoot about to hand over anything of worth to this bunch of loons. Allowing twenty minutes to come up with any sense was twenty minutes well spent, mainly because he knew twenty years wouldn't produce anything worthy of note. It would, however, give him the opportunity to record a level of negotiation and consultation that his elders and betters expected.

Three hours later, they started to filter back into the room and found him snoozing in his Merodian chair. In addition to the skipper being asleep, they were also fascinated by the chair with all of the buttons and switches, so took it upon themselves to choose a candidate to best poke and prod whilst the boss snored like a snorting warthog. Amongst the buttons stood out a large, round, red switch with the cross of Dalhag on it, a sign only associated with trouble and strife. Clearly, this was the button to press. Toestump was chosen as his idea it was that had bought them some time which sent them from the room, which bought them some time, which sent him to sleep, which bought them some time to create some good old-fashioned fun.

Dalhag had been named as the most feared man ever to have lived in Bellsurp, not because of a particularly nasty streak or a manner to stir feelings of hate and anger but because his creations were scandalously dangerous. They included such masterpieces as the baby spinner and the haemorrhoid snapper, but more importantly, the self-destruction button, which was big and red and bore his insignia. The cross of Dalhag.

Toestump's first move brought about a number of giggles and much squeaking of shoes, compelling him to backtrack until the mirth had subsided, although the giggles never actually disappeared, just reduced to a level associated with naughty boys outside of the headmaster's office. Swamsoot rolled peacefully in the Merodian chair as though rocked by light, soothing music, and the group stared cheekily at one another, cherishing each moment as though attending the clown's convention of the universe. Using some initiative, Toestump decided to remove at least one of the distractions by levitating to six inches above the floor and hovering towards the snoozing Swamsoot as the group tittered inanely.

As if being watched by one of the many Gods the Bellsurpians worshipped, flying Bellsurpians were normally coupled with flatulence and this was no exception, Toestump expelling a rattler. Swamsoot's eyes flashed open just as the floating soldier's hand slipped across the path of his knees.

"What in Tronk's name are you doing?" he screamed, bringing his hand down and his knee up at the same time, trapping Toestump in an excruciating arm-lock before throwing him to the floor, leaving only a pungent smell. "How many times do I have to tell you the chair is not a toy?" Feeling thoroughly admonished, the whole team started crying, reducing Swamsoot to a guilt-wracked jumble. Only time would tabulate that the complete crew and ship had been saved by a flying fart, but for now, he decided to adjourn proceedings until they composed themselves. That night, his diary would record his attempts to involve his best men to no avail, although his recording of the 'almost incident' would go unnoticed, as Bellsurpians believed that only things that happened *actually* happened. If they didn't happen, they weren't worthy of discussion. Theoretically, they weren't nearly annihilated.

Swamsoot made a mental note to speak to either Tam Wilson or Jack when they eventually landed about the difference in priorities between Earthlings and Bellsurpians.

Below them, meanwhile, Tam climbed out of bed and marched feverishly to the bathroom, where he carried out his regular ablutions before opening the back door to afford Jack the same luxury. Scratching themselves like flee-ridden grizzlies, both man and dog began frantically searching for food, knowing another long, laborious day stretched out ahead of them.

"That's the problem with the island of Scroat, Jack. Nothing new ever happens and nobody ever comes to visit." Jack, being a dog, had no idea what Tam had said, but Jack, being a dog, remembered the strange visitors the previous night and hoped they'd be back. He wouldn't be disappointed.

Come for Breakfast, Stay for Tea

Before leaving Bellsurp, Swamsoot had read all of the safety leaflets aboard the new vessel, appropriately named 'The Daftest', and painted all manner of stripes and colours. Not unlike other phrases, the name was one of many with a different Earth meaning, although the colours shocked even the most Bellsurpian of Bellsurpians. It had been decreed, however, that the best way to make an impression was to be noticed from a thousand gortanties and be proud of your display.

Had the shroud of invisibility not denied that type of view to everyone, many more people would indeed have seen them coming and may well have impressed them. Good old-fashioned fear ensured the invisibility shroud remained in place and only when they were confident the Earth people presented no threat would it be removed. For now, all that Swamsoot was concerned about was making the right and proper interaction with the right and proper people, which would, in turn, mean the crusade would be on track for success. Back home on Bellsurp, the news would soon be filtering through on the whiz-rod and a collection of reactions would soon be filtering back, ranging from congratulations to spits of jealousy. The hairs on his palms began to prickle with pride, reminding him to visit the hand barber.

Most of his instructions had been routinely vague and the envelope in which they were secreted was carefully marked to guarantee it wasn't opened until the ship was well past the point of return. A large proportion of the commands were simple reminders of what to bring home, including flowers, sweeties and any cute toys they managed to apprehend on this terrifying, dangerous mission. Remaining instructions, though, related to the need to bring back information and scientific data to enable the progress of a race with a need to develop at a pace at least equivalent to its nearest neighbours on the planet Jones.

Although much of the prerequisites were vitally important to the scientific extravagance of Bellsurp's finest scientists, Swamsoot had unilaterally decided that this mission would be special for his own reasons. Using his charm and well-travelled erudition, he would make contact with the finest of people, including breeding of refinement and class in abundance. This task complete, he would find a wife. It would mean doing what no Bellsurpian had ever done, even the travellers to Longstop in the galaxy of Plentitotti came home as single and frustrated astronauts, but Swamsoot had made a promise to both his mother and to himself before he left to himself because he genuinely believed he deserved a better life instead of being so accommodating to the battalion to whom he had already given so much. To his mother because she was sick of doing his washing.

"Try and find a wife while you're gone, son," she told him as though pleading with the refuse collector to take the bag full of dog sick as well. "Otherwise, I'll end up keeping you until you're one thousand years old."

Smiling sweetly before he left, he told her honestly. "Just make sure all of my underpants are clean when I return." They had an understanding, and although neither one actually understood what the understanding was, they managed to get along without attempting to kill one another. Except for the great bombing campaign of the old people's community hall on the Festival of Dallyport, he had never tried to kill his mother and she appreciated this so much that she barely poisoned his food at all these days. It was not a unique relationship in Bellsurp, but it was a relationship of mother and son that no one dared to come between.

On his desk before him, Swamsoot had spread out the rules of engagement between any Bellsurpian and any non-Bellsurpian and most of it made sense. That said, a great big chunk of it made no sense whatsoever, even to a man of his intelligence and his best known of home-spun competencies, was the ability to make sense of Bellsurpian nonsense. Before they could land to engage the locals of Scroat, they had to make sure they understood what was expected of them as ambassadors of their part of the universe.

Last night's foray had proved useful, but in fairness, it had been carried out on a whim and in a moment's light-headed madness. That they had managed to take anything worthwhile from the venture was not just a bonus; it was a positive miracle. This meant a lot to Bellsurpians because positive miracles were few and far between, certainly compared to the negative miracles for which many a catastrophe was blamed. If anyone was going to take credit for last night's success, he would have to discover whether or not *he* could formally claim it or whether it would have to be passed to one of his subordinates and recorded as a lucky shot. An hour of reading up on protocols would resolve that one and then they would have to prepare to land again. For what seemed like the fiftieth time, he prepared to call his troops together once more.

"Toestump," he said to his most trusted Calistone. "How many times have I tried to call the troops together today?"

"Fifty, sir," Toestump answered with an assured tone, the way he did most things, thus endearing himself further to the skipper.

"Really?" Swamsoot replied knowingly.

"Fifty," Toestump pre-emptively answered the next question.

"And how many times have I been unsuccessful?" The lack of further response gave it away. "Right then. Fifty-one it shall not become. Get the crew ready to land and if anyone tries to escape, make them listen to Batty and Batty talking about their family lives." Toestump looked shocked. Not familiar with irony or sarcasm, his inability to understand this particular train of thought bemused him.

"Certainly, sir. Shall I prepare Batty and Batty as well, sir?"

Swamsoot cast his eyes upward like an astronaut wondering if his last pair of cast-off underpants might be floating in the ether. "No need to do that, Toestump. If there's one thing they don't need, it's preparation to talk about themselves. In fact, if ever a pair could talk without breathing, Batty and Batty are that pair, although they would probably then make up another story about the day they talked without breathing."

"I think they'd die if they tried it on Earth, sir. Although, I do know a number of Bellsurpians who can do it whilst standing on their cousins, who in turn are underwater."

"Yes," Swamsoot mentioned casually. "I remember the televised championships, which was a real boon for the sport. How many Bellsurpians were killed during that tournament, Toestump?"

"None, sir, although a number of the horses they were riding were never seen again."

"Sad. Sad indeed, especially if you're a horse, or a horse trainer, or a horse owner, or a horse's head keeper. It really was a bad day for horses."

"The worst in televisual history. I believe, sir."

"What about the national swinging horse combat challenge? Didn't that have a bad return of competitors?"

"Yes, sir, but a lot of horses were rescued from the trees, sir." Toestump's refreshing honesty filled the captain with mixed emotions. At some stage in the future, they might have to use some Bellsurpian charm to fend off vitriolic humans and lies may be a necessary evil. It was a real concern to a man who hailed from a race that couldn't lie to save their lives. In an attempt to acclimatise themselves on the way to Earth, he had tried to get them to partake in a lying competition, with rules and parameters laid down by him.

"All lying must be completely believable and not beyond the realms of understanding. All lies must be backed up with another, more detailed lie should there be a need for clarification by non-believers or anyone who simply wishes to start a fight because they don't believe you. OK then, let's get started." Before he had realised what he had said, the room had cleared in case someone *had* wanted a fight and it took another two days and fifteen explanations to get them back into the room.

Interminable cowardice did not seem out of place on Bellsurp, but Swamsoot was always perplexed by its power to turn a warrior into a blubbering wreck, although the literal Bellsurpian translation of warrior meant 'he who cries like a baby'. If he had been given a chance to do it his way, the crew would have been made up of stout-hearted creatures of iron and steel, as opposed to the limp-wristed creatures of tissue and tepid water. All in all, though, his team verged on the satisfactory and he wouldn't have swapped them for any others on his planet, with the obvious exception of the women he yearned for and the people who could string words together without falling over.

Once more, the time had come to brief the landing party and he had left word with his commanders to bring them together in a formal gathering. Waking up to the information that they had carried out his instructions to the letter confounded him only because he couldn't remember writing any such letter. Nonetheless, he splashed some water on his face and walked swiftly to the conference room, where they stood to attention in silence. Silence from a collective was very rare and he wondered if everything was OK.

"Yes, everything is fine, sir," Toestump assured him from just within thought-shot.

"Really? How splendid."

Hushed serenity bellowed out from the team before him and he felt at peace with them all. "Yes, how very splendid this is that you have all arrived on time..." he checked his watch and noticed he had been asleep for four hours since he requested their presence. "Oh well! Now that you are all here and resplendent in uniform, I shall run briefly through our remit and plans. Any questions before I start?" Of the sixty people present, sixty-four hands were raised to take up the quizzical offer. "Any questions that do not relate to fighting the locals?" No more than ten hands were left aloft. "Or questions that don't relate to what time it gets dark?" With the room now bereft of upright limbs, he continued with a flurry. "I have received a message on the Danatronical starflash from the king, commending us for the sterling work so far achieved on this momentous trip across the vast fields of giddy black. I shall read it to you all.

'Captain Swamsoot. May I commend you and your crew for all of the sterling work so far achieved on the momentous trip across the vast fields of giddy black.'

"And that is from the King. There is a PS which reads *'Please read this to everyone."*

To a man etc., there wasn't a dry eye in the house, such was the emotion tied up in the message from the only king that they had any time for. Stinted whispers could be heard around the room.

"I bet he wrote it himself."

"They don't make them like him anymore."

"He truly is the King who speaks from the heart."

"Does he have a mouth on his heart?"

"I wasn't really paying attention. What did he say?"

Swamsoot, feeling pride rushing through his veins, added his own emotional attestation to proceedings. "He's a nice man, the king, isn't he?" Nods and grunts affirmed his view and he moved on swiftly. "So, the plan is to go and visit the same pair of humans and try to establish exactly what their role is on the island. We know one of them rules the place, but we aren't sure which one; however, the small hairy one does tend to have a look of regal status about him, although I'm not absolutely sure what that means. Once we've determined which one the leader is, we will begin to sell the necessary materials to enable our trip to be declared a run-away success." Sixty-four hands flew skywards. "That does not mean we have to run away." Sixty-four hands returned to their respective sides and backs. "What we cannot have on this sortie is anyone trying to sell anything without full written consent. Anyone trying to cut corners will be dealt with by the full power of the law back on Bellsurp. Are you all clear on what is expected of you?" Sixty-four hands appeared. "Have you all read your indoctrination literature?" Sixty-four hands remained airborne but wavering slightly. "The little pieces of paper that were pushed under your bedroom doors?" Ten hands remained upright. "Or slipped into your sleeping boxes? Splendid. Everyone should know what to do then. Any questions about detail should be directed to Toestump before we land and I look forward to a very successful trip with results we will be proud to send across the millions of gortanties on the Danatronical starflash. Without further delay, let's climb on board and sing like Massimals." Four hands appeared with shaking urgency. "Yes, what is it?" After a short discussion, one of the hand owners was delegated the task of asking the question.

"Sir, do we have to sing like Massimals too?"

"Yes, you Massimals have to sing like Massimals too. Right, let's go to Earth and rock the joint." Nobody knew what that meant, but such was the faith in their man that they followed him all the same. Within an hour, the landing craft was loaded and in the air for the short trip to Tam Wilson's place, where he sat in the garden talking to Jack, unaware he was again to be visited by a mysterious group of people from a planet he had never heard of.

Somehow, however, Jack knew.

Don't Confuse Them

"If I was a dog, would you find me attractive, Jack?" Whilst sniffing his genitals, Jack would have found the world's ugliest frog attractive by comparison, but his incomprehension of the English language meant the sniffing continued unabated. "I know it's not the type of question you'd be expected to answer in a court of law, but I'm sure I'm not the most unattractive man on the island. So why do I appear to be the only man on the island without a life partner, present company excepted and a real need for human companionship?" Jack lifted his head, slightly woozy from the odour he had inflicted upon himself and smiled a doggy smile at his master. In recognition of Jack looking cute, Tam put out his hand to offer a stroke of comfort, to which Jack duly approached and accepted. Both man and dog started at each other with conflicting thoughts.

I bet you would sacrifice yourself for me if the need arose because that's what a man's best friend does, Tam thought.

I wish you'd scratch a bit harder, Jack thought, then immediately turned his thoughts to the piece of bacon rind left on Tam's plate.

"If I had a woman, Jack, the days would seem fresher and happier and we would eat healthier, mainly because that's the type of thing that women make us do. I don't want someone to come in and tell us what we can and can't do, of course, but it would be nice to have someone to walk with other than you my friend. It would be nice to have someone we could spoil a little bit, wouldn't it? A pretty person, although they don't have to be pretty, as long as they don't smell, unless it's a nice perfume type of smell. You wouldn't understand that part, Jack, but the nicest smell in the world is the smell of a woman when she has that perfume stuff on her and it leaves a trail when she walks around the house. Naturally, we don't want the smell to be too strong, just in case it lands on our clothes and fur because we don't want the lads in the pub thinking we've turned a bit soft. Mind you, young David Burns wears an after-shave and the lasses in the village can't get enough of him. And, it doesn't appear to bother them that he hasn't actually started shaving yet."

Feeling in an obvious sombre mood, Tam sat back on his garden bench and watched the light breeze sweeping in from The Irish Sea and shaking the grass in his patch that was probably two or three days overgrown. It was another of those things that a woman would have reminded him to do instead of him simply heading off to the pub every morning and every night. What Tam really needed in his life was some order and as he pondered the unlikeness of someone, anyone, coming into his life at this stage, he was consumed with a feeling of melancholy soberness. It may have been simply down to the fact that he was sober for the first time in a month, but moreover, it was probably down to his failure to be able to maintain a relationship with anyone other than his dog.

"Jack, I need some company other than yours," he said and dropped his head to his chest. "And if I don't find some soon, I think I'm going to go mad."

"Good morning, you complete buffoon," Swamsoot said with a mode of confidence that belied a man so small in physical stature. "You probably thought you were going to sit around keeping your money today, but that's because you're too stupid to think otherwise. Let's be fair, it's a genuine mystery that you're able to think at all, but I'm just the man to help you out and offer you the most overpriced pile of rubbish you've ever seen."

Tam sat up and looked at the crowd of people invading his land. "Ahem. Good morning to you…" A hushed silence fell momentarily between them all. "What did you call me?"

Swamsoot wasn't remotely fazed. "Believe me, what I've called you so far has no bearing on what I'll be calling you after you've bought this pile of trash I have here to overcharge you for, you blithering numbskull." The wise captain moved straight in to ascertain the necessary information. "However, if you don't have the authority to make such decisions…" His slow and purposeful look towards Jack seemed downright peculiar, made only more so by Jack's now apparent insatiable appetite for his own testicles. Swamsoot smiled knowingly at man and dog, then turned his attention to the sale once more. "What I have here is a machine that you are not bright enough to use, but you'll undoubtedly pay over the odds for, mainly because you're as dozy as a daft donkey who's just won the daftest donkey prize on daft donkey day." With that, he produced a tiny battery-shaped metallic implement and proceeded to shake it at Tam, who sat motionless as his dog continued to eat himself from the privates upwards.

"I see!" ventured the Scotsman, confounded by the strange young man trying to sell him a metal 'thing'.

"Actually, I'm surprised that you're able to say that with any conviction, such is your loose grasp on reality and sense."

"Yes."

"Although you might be simply carrying out orders and presenting a façade of ridiculous behaviour in order to appease your masters and chiefs."

"Yes," Tam repeated. "I think I'll have a drink. Would you, or any of your wee friends, care for a drink of… water? I'm afraid I don't have anything else for people of your age or size." Jack stood up quickly when Tam moved and the attention suddenly turned totally to him.

"Is he telling the truth?" Swamsoot quizzed the dog meaningfully and felt strangely cheated when Jack wagged his tail and followed Tam through the door to the kitchen. There was no disguising the fact that Jack was more comfortable with the Bellsurpians than Tam was and the Calistones sensed it.

"The small hairy one seems pleased that we're here, sir," Toestump mentioned dutifully. "Although he does also seem to have an unhealthy infatuation with his loins and his bottom, sir."

"Yes, Toestump," Swamsoot answered pensively. "I noticed that myself. I wonder if it's some kind of tactic to put us off his scent."

"The scent of his loins and his bottom, sir?"

"It's a figure of speech, Toestump."

"I see, sir." Toestump lied, blushing slightly in case of any of his breed were close enough to check his mind.

"I think," Swamsoot continued with a short pause. "That he, the small hairy one, is leading us down a route of confusion to enable his subordinate to act out some kind of fantasy, probably because of an unpaid debt." The route of confusion quickly caught up with his crew members, with them all suddenly appearing as drunk as drunken goats on a goat's end-of-season football trip. "Perhaps we should give them a little breathing space and make our exit as quickly as possible." And in an instant, they had all left the area as swiftly as they had arrived. In the kitchen, Tam struggled to make any sense of the small altercation with the boy with the nice skin and the sharp tongue. Jack, however, had returned to his favourite position and was once more upside down dealing with genitalia.

"Do you think I should offer them something to eat, Jack?" asked the benevolent Scotsman. As any obedient dog would, Jack lifted his head momentarily and wagged his tail at the sound of his name being uttered by his master. "Well, I suppose it would be rude not to, wouldn't it? I'll ask them if they like fried eggs and toast." Jack stood up and followed Tam back to the garden to find the place bereft of strangers before checking indoors. Both man and dog stared blankly at the space and then at each other as though waiting for an explanation. In the corner of the room stood a large oak bureau with two enormous, ox-shaped bookends jamming one solitary book between them. Tam moved gingerly towards it and checked to see if his visitors had slid in behind the piece of furniture, the way children sometimes do for fun. "Not there, boy," he told his best friend and scratched his head ruefully as his mind raced at the thought of that many youths disappearing so quickly and began wondering if they had actually ever been here. Beneath his feet, the old red and blue rug stuck to his soles and he reminded himself to throw it out and buy a new one in case the visitors came back. "We don't get many people coming to see us, do we, Jack?" he mentioned casually, as he carried on searching for the youngsters. "So, I think it's only polite that we make a show for them and offer them something nice to eat… provided they come out of their hiding place… I don't want to have to search for ever…" His rising volume was clearly for the sake of any would-be in-hiding sorts, but all of his oral jousting was in vain, as they stayed out of sight until he was too bored to look further. "Rather strange that, Jack. I would have thought they might have wanted to hang around a little longer to see what happens on…" he looked at the calendar next to the wide-screen television. "Saturdays. After all, I might just be able to throw some light on the culture and background of this island." In the light fitting above him, the recording device picked up every sound. "I am the island dignitary, so to speak and everyone who…"

"Hello, again, you idiots," Swamsoot noted as he walked through the door. "So, as the island dignitary, you should certainly be able to make the type of decisions we need and in return, I will give you something completely worthless and charge you a fortune. But not because I like you, moreover because I think you are stupid enough to fall for it. Dopey." Tam examined the youthful Swamsoot and his entourage of small, quieter friends.

"Who do you belong to, exactly and how long are you here for?"

"The princely high-born family, of course, and we're here for the length of time it takes, whether that be a day or a meddlimant."

"A meddi what?"

"Mant, you idiot, but a simple lesson from me could give you the wealth of knowledge you require to be able to master the basics of existence, you moron."

"Could you stop calling me names… by the way, what is your name?"

"Damalgo Winstonian Swamsoot. What's your name, thicko?"

"Thomas Alexander Wilson and stop it, will you, or I'll put you over my knee." Toestump sidled up to his captain and whispered carefully.

"He's losing his temper, sir."

"Really. Perhaps he's highly strung, the way a lot of human Royals appear to be when they posture. Do you remember that story I told you about that, Henry the Eighth, who kept on killing women because he had lost his socks?"

A general murmur of situation appreciation rolled across the room. Tam watched carefully as the congregation congregated to concur with the sentiment of the aforementioned royal and he smiled to himself as a warm, contentment entered his soul for the first time in a long time. As hard as he tried, Tam Wilson could not remember how long it had been since he last had company. These strange, ill-mannered youths had come to his home uninvited on two separate occasions and insulted him and he was delighted. For years, the people of Scroat had seen him as a cantankerous old soul, although nobody could remember meeting him sober. Inevitably, visitors were few and far between. These youths, though, seemed unperturbed by his general demeanour, instilling in him a sense of confidence and zest.

"Who wants a drink?" he suddenly shouted as if to demonstrate his happiness.

"Toestump. See if you can find the answer to that for this idiot," Swamsoot demanded, then slipped back into selling mode seamlessly. "If you were to take what I have to offer, I can guarantee a period of time so small that it will make no difference to your lifestyle in any way. However, being as dim as you are, it won't make a bit of difference whether or not you so much as understand what I want you to buy."

Tam felt a smile part his lips; the type of smile that can't be disguised and usually accompanies the first-time older members of a family discover your first girlfriend and denial is pointless.

"OK then," he said casually. "I'll buy it." Swamsoot's complexion turned from excited anticipation to pure confusion, the way a fish looks as the hook is removed and it finds itself back in the water and not a frying pan.

"Buy what?" he asked Tam.

"Whatever you're selling, son." Tam appeared caught up in a game with children who were, momentarily at least, making him feel currently congenial and his mood flashed a signal for the Calistones.

"Sir," Toestump whispered to the confused captain. "He appears to be very happy about something."

"Yes, I noticed that Toestump, although I can't imagine what it is."

"I'll tell you what I'll do," Tam said with a tone as giddy as a girl accepting a dance at the school disco from the gorgeous physics teacher. "You can carry on making up whatever it is you want to sell me and I'll go and make some pop. It'll have to be the stuff you dilute because I don't have any fizzy pop. Is that OK?"

The group looked at Swamsoot for direction but the best he could do was return the look of mystification with interest. It was a shot in the dark, but a gamble he decided worth taking and so spat it out.

"Yes," he answered confidently. Clearly, the years of training as a skipper of a multifunctional, space-hopping, intergalactic, flying planet had paid dividends and Tam replied graciously.

"Good! Put the telly on if you want while I'm in the kitchen. There might be some kids' programmes on that you can watch before you have to do a bunk." A look to his right let him know that his team were already tracing the meaning of 'doing a bunk', and as Tam walked to the kitchen, he beckoned them all to his side.

"Let's not panic because we never expected this to be easy. This might get dangerous and this human man is clearly brighter than we give him credit for, although none of our data has them clever enough to keep up this pretence for long."

Snide

Battleprop looked at the data from the computer banks and smiled as he read the line that repeated over and again.

HUMANS APPEAR TO BE A LOWER FORM OF LIFE AND ARE LIGHT YEARS BEHIND BELLSURP IN EVOLUTIONARY TERMS.

Just Stay Away From the Bottle

Most of the landing party were now in tears and his first reaction was to hand out handkerchiefs in an attempt to stem the flow of tears. "We can't let him see we're not fighting material, otherwise he'll eat us alive." Bad choice of words, he deduced, as the tears were accompanied by mild screaming. "It's a turn of phrase used by humans. They don't actually eat…" The pause for consideration of that option was too much of a giveaway and within seconds, he was alone in the room.

"Who wants orange and who wants elderberry?" shouted the Scottish voice from the kitchen. The lack of response brought him back in to see his visitors almost all missing again. "I use the elderberry juice to keep me regular, but it is quite tasty. Where's everyone gone then?"

Swamsoot fleetingly paused.

"They've had to go for things," he said brilliantly. "And might be gone for some time."

"Their Mothers probably told them what time to be back, eh? As chance would have it, my mother used to tell me I had to come back home every hour on the hour when we were on holiday. I presume you're all staying at the holiday cottages?"

"Do you?" Swamsoot answered with Bellsurpian innocence.

"Funny, but I never knew they were letting them again."

"Letting them do what?" but Tam had switched off.

"So, do you want orange or elderberry, son?" A trait of Bellsurp was to quizzically scratch when faced with something of stupefaction and being referred to as son stupefied him greatly. Scratching like a lop-ridden baboon, he answered luckily.

"The same as you would be fine." Tam produced a drink of orange juice in a glass, dirty enough to be a find in the dustbin of the island's dirtiest café.

"So where are you from then, son?" he asked when he sat down after dutifully placing the glass on a small table in front of the guest. Swamsoot scratched and responded with confidence.

"Up there, today," he replied, pointing skyward.

Tam was tickled by the reply. "And what about before today, son?" he continued with a small giggle forming deep in his throat.

"Further up there," Swamsoot answered with an unerring conviction and a seeming propensity for scratching. "We intend to sell you an enormous amount of nothing for a price you wouldn't dream of spending if you were anything other than dopey. And don't try and tell me dopey isn't a word because it entered the word reference guidebook a number of years ago."

"Dictionary." Tam helped him out.

Learning new words was one of the space traveller's weaknesses and he touched his right foot as a reminder; the way he always touched his foot to remember something new. "Dactionary, yes."

"No," Tam corrected. "I said dictionary." Repeating the word with the same accent made it no easier for his visitor.

"So did I." One brief pronunciation lesson later, the leader of travelling Bellsurpians was clear in his dictionary definition and enunciation. A nice, friendly détente had emerged and to celebrate the relationship, Swamsoot looked carefully at his orange juice, whereupon it disappeared from the glass and simultaneously lodged itself softly in his stomach. Tam noticed the incident, or at least thought he noticed, but had the good grace not to mention it to his new, youthful friend.

"So, how long are you here for…? I still don't know your name, son."

"Damalgo Winstonian Swamsoot. I mentioned it earlier."

"So that's your real name? Where on Earth did you get a name like that Damalgo Winstonian Swamsoot?"

"Oh no," replied the spaceman curtly. "Nowhere on Earth."

Tam nodded at the smart answer. "Well, I'll call you Dammy. I bet all of your friends call you Dammy, do they?" The well-balanced skipper pondered the notion before answering apolitically and aping his host.

"Yes, they do… I don't know your name, son."

Tam balked slightly. "Mr Wilson, but if you stop being so clever, you can call me Tam." Both man and boyish-looking man sat back in their respective chairs with an uneasy feeling about how the conversation should proceed, but both were strangely content to be sharing this mutuality. Swamsoot struggled to deal with the next line of the sale with the instruction to stop being as clever and

Tam was simply happy to be in the company of what he thought was another human being.

The large mahogany clock on the mantelpiece ticked heavily, though with a soothing, melodic regularity that appealed to each of the coteries as they stared in every available direction. A painting of a swan adorned the long wall between the kitchen door and the exit to the front of the building and the frame showed signs of wear and tear.

"That's an interesting piece." Swamsoot noticed casually.

"Yes, my father painted that when he was a young man. He went to university in Edinburgh a long time ago and could have been a world-renowned painter, but for the snobbery that goes with…" The feeling of him falling into a tirade pattern halted him in his tracks.

"What does your father do, Dammy?"

"He passes through black holes and actively seeks out the lost tribes from various cultures to try and rekindle the refinement that may once have made their people a force or a worthy contemporary for the universe to hold precious."

"I see," Tam replied slowly as if just having watched his last chip get off the plate and walk out of the door. "So, does he like football?"

"It's not a concept he's familiar with, Tam."

Suddenly, Tam was unsure that this new friend was going to be as much fun as he had anticipated. "We do have a number of pastimes that he does indulge in when he's home, but as he only arrives home every fourth green moon, it isn't the top of his list of things to do."

"I don't suppose it would be if he only comes home once in a fourth green moon. They don't come around too often, do they?"

"Every Dintopat on Bellsurp. How often do they come around here?"

Tam smiled at the level of nonsensical chat this youth could indulge in. "Not that often Dammy, in fact, there are those who claim to have never seen a green moon, but they don't even believe it's made of cheese."

"Every meddlimant, my family rake up enough ground creatures to make the moon sacrifice and we throw it at the furthest away one."

"Really?" Tam asked nonsensically.

"And if we ever reach it, we'll get to land the Mescitow on the Landibot or the Landibot on the Mescitow."

"You don't say?" responded the increasingly excitable Scot. During his younger days, he had been a dedicated follower of Monty Pythons Flying Circus and the sensation of slipping into absurdity-mode tickled him. Sadly, the enjoyment of it was lost on the youthful-looking Swamsoot, who was speaking from the heart on matters of great family pride. Back on Bellsurp, moon targeting was a national disport and those who refrained from joining in were classed as snobs or weaklings. To Tam, though, the notion of chucking things at the moon had hilarious potential and his old-school pals would be proud of the debate. Even the old clock on the mantelpiece seemed to be ticking quicker at the prospect of the nonsense. Only when he listened more carefully did he realise the clock *was* actually ticking quicker than normal and the hands were racing around the face like greyhounds in pursuit of a plump hare.

"What the devil is wrong with that?" asked the bemused host as he stood up and walked towards the mysterious timepiece. "It's never done that before."

Swamsoot stood up and followed him to the mantle. "Oh, it's made from functional mechanics. That will be me making it speed up then, with the over active electron gland, which really is the bane of the Swamsoot clan. It's a little embarrassing, really, although I know I can't do anything about it and I shouldn't be embarrassed by it, but I am what I am."

Tam looked quizzically at him. "You are what you are what?"

"Just what I am, the way we all are what we are. You're not ashamed of being asinine, are you?"

Tam's inner dictionary frequently let him down. "I'm not really sure, actually."

"Well, there you are. Most of the Swamsoot clan have difficulties with modular mechanics, although some of my more impertinent relatives try to play down the electronic thing. If it was up to me, I'd make it a skill and introduce it to the local educational curriculum. Inextricable individuals like yourself could only benefit from this type of forward-thinking, a far cry from your ineptitude deemed acceptable by the masses of dimwits of your ilk."

Tam smiled sweetly, "I see. And would you like another drink?"

"It has some appeal, I have to say, but it may be more prudent to make this sale here and now and receive the acclaim I deserve." After a moment's ponder, Swamsoot grudgingly corrected himself. "And the crew, of course."

Tam looked at Jack for some inspiration on how to join in with this conversation, which seemed to be taking on a life of its own. Ordinarily, although not always the most eloquent of individuals, he could mix it with most wordsmiths without too much pause for thought between contentious points. For now, however, he stood agog as this youngster spoke a type of slang that boggled his mind.

He thought about American films from years before when some of the foreign drivel he and his friends were force-fed had their heads spinning like washing machines hooked on rinse. What he also remembered was that he and his friends picked up all of the 'jive' and soon thereafter used it as frequently as they used their index fingers for nose clearance.

Perhaps this type of 'speak' was the new 'jive' and within minutes, he would cotton on and understand everything currently catalogued under the gibberish titles. Within minutes he was close to tears and imploring Swamsoot to shut up.

"If I knew what it was you were saying, then perhaps we could… well, I don't know what we could do actually, but I'm rather afraid that if you don't explain exactly what it is you're talking about, I'm afraid I'll have to ask you to leave."

Swamsoot was astonished at this move towards aggression and immediately took evasive action. "Right then, I'll double the price and give you half of what I originally said I'd give you. Do we have a deal?" Suddenly, as if struck by a blinding light, it all became so clear to Tam, who perked up at the discovery. His ears vibrated gently, a trait associated with the Wilson family for generations and even the usually unflappable Swamsoot noticed the outrageous lobe-shake was less than the norm, even for a race as downwardly mobile as humans.

Travelling over a million Gortanties is always a task, even for the most perspicacious of space commuters and humour had been a precious commodity. In preparation for the onslaught, he had managed to watch an inordinate amount of classic comedies, with a particular penchant for Laurel and Hardy and laughter was not easy for Bellsurpians. Now, however, after watching ears shake like humming bird's wings on a good drying day,

Swamsoot felt obliged to laugh out loud. Naturally, this simply confirmed Tam's premise that the visitor was on a trip from a loony bin.

"I'm sorry, son, but you're on one of the trips from the mainland, aren't you, from one of those… special hospitals?" Unfortunately, the ears continued to wave like a pair of door chimes, sending the space man into further convulsions. "I've got nothing against you or the trips to the island, but to be honest, I'm not convinced you should be here without your… what do you call the people who look after you?"

Swamsoot repressed his mild hilarity. "Servants."

Tam grimaced. "I mean, what do you call the carers… Hang on! That's what they're called, isn't it?"

For no obvious reason, a searing pain of uneasiness now existed between them, but only Tam was concerned by it. Swamsoot had expected such a relationship to materialise at some stage and, as he was still ahead of plan, remained completely unperturbed by it.

"I'm amazed that you were able to put a tag on them in any event, being as speaking also requires a modicum of intelligence. Should you wish to buy what I have to sell, though, we could be in a position to strike up a deal to benefit both you and me. Obviously, me more than you, but that goes without saying because of the intelligence gap." Tam's apprehension began to get the better of him and he could feel the need to end the conversation and show this young boy the door, regardless of the fact he had admittedly been pleased to accept him and his friends into his home. Being a curious type, though, he didn't dare ask him to leave until he discovered who he was and what the hell he was talking about.

"Just as a matter of interest," he conjectured. "Who are you and what the hell are you talking about?"

Swamsoot grinned. "Isn't it obvious? Oh no, it clearly isn't obvious to you because you're not terribly bright. If you were to purchase what I have to sell, however, this minor detail of a make-up flaw could be overcome with the minimum of disruption to your lifestyle. Plus, of course, your contemporaries will no longer look at you as though you are inferior to them, as well as the end of all ridicule to your face in addition to what goes on in your absence."

Tam was affected the way a wasp is affected when a complete stranger tries to hit it with a newspaper. "What do you mean, what goes on in my absence? Are that lot calling me behind my back?"

"My dear man." Swamsoot started with the look of a man staring smugly over the top of his spectacles. "People all over the place call you and laugh at you. Weren't you aware?" Tam shrugged his shoulders with a mixture of apathy and dread. "Hardly anyone does anything other than call you. If you decide to buy my wonder stuff, your life would be transformed almost immediately."

Without pause for thought, Tam realised a missing link. "How old are you, son?"

"Few hundred of your years, I suppose, although I'd have to do the sums."

"Have you left school yet?"

"Yes."

"When?"

"Often."

"When was the last time?"

"That doesn't make sense. You appear to have missed a few words out there, but my goods will resolve your inability to complete a sentence in any meaningful way."

Tam growled, almost angrily. "Just answer the question and where are your friends while I remember?"

"Where are my friends while you remember what?"

"I've read about this type of thing where one of them distracts the mark while the others creep in and steal the family silver. Right then, don't move."

Being of sound mind and body, as well as six or seven stone lighter than Tam, Swamsoot agreed and duly sat motionless whilst the officious Scot ransacked his own home in search of intruders.

It wasn't a process the space traveller was completely unfamiliar with due to a home-bred version from Bellsurp whereby anyone deemed to be unfit to breed small animals called Wengers were searched upon request of a breeding licence. Only those with sufficient dust in personal places were authorised to begin the laborious process of multiplying the Wenger population, which was never popular with the animal's critics. Wenger haters constantly carped about the Wenger carping, but as they were bred as hunting and moaning beasts, the carping continued and the Wenger community increased unabated. Searches such as the one Tam was undertaking, however, seemed downright odd. Dust searchers set about their work with vigour and verve, never wavering from their objectives and being clear in their aims and objectives. Tam was on his hands and knees, looking under furniture and calling out unfamiliar words.

"If I find ye, I'll rip yer skibbard from yer reeky." It was neither Scottish nor human but a simple invention of wailing noises intended to scare trespassers from their lairs, much like the bagpipe.

Looking up at Swamsoot, Tam noticed a shimmering effect across his body as the young man started to disappear before his eyes. A cold-looking shadow flashed slowly and indistinctly from his head to his toes and the potential con artist began to fade away. Tam rubbed his eyes and pleaded silently for corroboration of events or assistance in his time of failing eyesight.

Neither came.

In addition, the mysterious events were compounded by a series of beeping noises accompanied by giggles and what sounded like flatulence. Swamsoot faded in and out of view like a mystifying mirage in his own living room and although this mirage effect wasn't the first time he had experienced such phenomena, this was the first time during sobriety. Within seconds, Swamsoot was joined by another youngster dressed in similar garb and immediately began speaking the same type of garbage.

"Sir, message from Bellsurp says we need to send visual images to verify the… erm… leader is actually the leader of his tribe."

"Certainly, Delius. Do you have the image collector?"

"Yes, sir," Delius answered with zest and produced a pocket-sized camera. "Shall I take the image now, sir?"

Swamsoot smiled a knowing smile. "Delius, It would hardly be protocol to capture the image of a king without first seeking permission, would it?"

"Absolutely, sir. Please forgive me." One hair ruffle later, the moment had been forgotten and Swamsoot turned his attention to his host, who still held his position on his knees, frantically rubbing his eyes.

"Am I still drunk and dreaming?" asked Tam, for the first time thinking a dream sequence might be in place. "If I am, can I roll over and have a different dream, please, now that I don't like what I'm seeing?"

Swamsoot and Delius looked on with a degree of disbelief, but having contended with Bellsurpian behaviour patterns for many years, weren't fazed by it all.

"What about if I sell you a dream that you like?" Swamsoot suggested with the smell of a sale in his nostrils. "I know it won't be any different to anything you have now, but wouldn't it be nice to have to pay for one that you don't want as opposed to simply… having one, I suppose?" Tam stopped sulking and whinging long enough to take in what had been said. Up until now, the day had been no more than a foray into a child's play time, where joining in was the order of the day, but suddenly a sinister sensation had crept up to bite him squarely on the backside.

"Who are you exactly?"

A reasonable question, Swamsoot thought. "Damalgo Winstonian Swamsoot, at your service, sir. I should point out, however, it's not so much at your service, more like a service seller, so to speak."

"Well said, sir," Delius agreed with the air of a man who wouldn't miss an opportunity for sycophancy when the chance uncovered itself.

"But exactly, who are you?" Tam reinvestigated, obviously not happy with the first attempt at an answer. "And I don't just mean your name."

Swamsoot rubbed his chin the way Bellsurpians had rubbed their chins for centuries. "I see," he noted dishonestly. "You want to know exactly who I am, as opposed to who I am exactly? Give me a moment, please," requested the confused skipper and turned ruefully to his right-hand man. "Do you think it's a trick, Delius?"

"I'm not sure, sir, but we have a number of Calistones nearby if you require confirmation, sir."

"Mmm. Let's get one of them in then and we'll try this out to see if it's a battle of wits. Do you remember the trip to Alsatataa where the inhabitants wanted to joust with our intellectual capacitators?"

"As though it was only a few days ago, sir." Before Swamsoot could respond, Delius realised it had indeed only been a few days before and he left the room to find a Calistone waiting at the door, already aware of what was required

"What is your reading of the situation?" Delius asked sternly, as though blaming the subordinate for his previous minor mishap with the boss.

"The man's an idiot, sir," answered the bright-faced Calistone without the merest hint of irony. "And before you ask, sir, I'm referring to the human."

"I see," mused Delius. "This is an interesting turn of events." And in a shake, he was back in the house alongside his skipper, reporting on the mind reader's view of happenings in the Wilson household. "Sir," he whispered to Swamsoot. "Apparently he's an idiot."

Swamsoot rubbed his chin softly. "Really? Now I wasn't expecting that. Could he possibly be fooling us into thinking he's an idiot, but he's actually a genius of some description?"

"I'll check straight away, sir," Delius replied and returned to find the waiting Calistone as eager as a beaver trying to impress his girlfriend's father.

"The man is an idiot, sir," reiterated the mind reader. "Although he does appear to have a thought in his head that I haven't before encountered." Delius returned with the relevant information and the two Bellsurpians watched carefully as Tam Wilson clambered to his feet, asking the same question.

"Please tell me who you are? And I don't just mean tell me your name because names don't mean anything to me, but I do need to know who you are and whether or not you're tricking me with devilment and treachery." But Swamsoot was more interested in what particular thought Tam had that his Calistone had never encountered.

Back on Bellsurp, alcohol had been banished for thousands of years and youngsters in their first few centuries had never seen or heard of its powers of sorcery. Being of soaked mind and body, this alcohol had the visitors baffled with its mind-bending skills, leaving the leader a problem to deal with.

"All right then," he suddenly blurted out with confidence. "My name is Damalgo Winstonian Swamsoot and I am the captain of a ship called… What ship did we come in, Delius?"

"The Wentaway, sir."

"Called the Wentaway and we have travelled nearly two million gortanties to arrive here where we can sell you whatever it is you wish to buy, just so long as you don't want it and we can sell it to you anyway. Or at least carry out the transaction to our advantage."

Tam moved across to his armchair and settled in it comfortably. "I see." Naturally, this information meant nothing to him and Swamsoot might as well have dispensed with the translation. "So why are you here?"

"Delius, check with the Calistone to see if the unrecognisable thought could be a strain of memory loss as he appears to be repeating himself." Delius duly obliged, but quickly returned with the negative response.

"Apparently not, sir. The Calistone thinks it may be linked to his Royal status, as it appears to give him a sense of strange confidence and boldness."

"Makes sense," Swamsoot noted with acceptance in his voice. "Can I ask you a question, your Royal Highness?" he enquired of the drunken Scot.

"Aye," Tam answered and waited whilst the two young men looked at him and then at each other.

"You what?" asked the skipper.

"What?" asked Tam with as much curiosity.

"I do apologise, your Highness, but you started to say something."

"No, I didn't."

"Yes, you did, just then."

"Are you mad?" Tam asked with a hint of vexation creeping into his voice.

"It could be a trick, sir," Delius mentioned casually. "Or even a test."

"Mmm. Fair point Delius! I'll keep going and see how it turns out. Your Highness, you started saying something by saying 'I', which I happen to know is how humans often start talking, especially when they are about to start talking about themselves. A lot of preparation has gone into this trip and information such as that was always going to be picked up by our researchers. Your politicians, for instance, always start sentences with that word before they start lying. They also start sentences with 'Let me answer that question in a different way', so as you can see, we know when you are about to start talking."

"I didn't say 'I'. I said 'aye', which is a completely different word."

Panic set in.

"Delius, go and check the dials to see if we're on the right planet. I don't recall Earth being this complicated." Swamsoot felt himself standing up and then sitting down, all in the same movement. How could 'I' and 'I' mean something different? Outside, the Calistones had picked up on his confusion and were running scared, as if trying to escape and hide from a scary, diseased bewilderment bug, none of which made any sense, but Calistones reacted to the fear of others. Delius had passed them by on his way back to the ship without so much as a sideways glance, unwittingly causing a stir of mistrust, which turned the Calistone's panic vibes into positive anarchy.

"Run!" someone shouted unnecessarily as everyone already had run in some direction.

"Hide!" shouted another without waiting for a reaction. Six of the crew ran directly into one another, causing a mixture of terror and hilarity and six more picked up on the vibe and assumed it to be best practice. Within seconds, forty-eight of the crew lay scattered around the area outside of Tam's house as though a huge bowling ball had skittled them like ninepins on a slippery surface.

Between the potential skull-breaking smashes, the noise of the howls of fear and fun caused Tam to stand up and take his hands down from his face. Immediately beneath his lounge window, a pile of bodies squirmed and grunted, generally causing a scene of disquiet that rendered him further confounded by what could only be described as odd. Swamsoot found himself bouncing on the armchair like an overweight acrobat on a piece of elastic, unable to control his confused state based only on a minor dialectic indiscretion. As calm as he wasn't, he managed to figure out this wasn't going to be good for the mission at large. Tam, on the other hand, seemed happy to be the one 'least' out of control, although competition for that particular title didn't appear to be too hotly contested. Delius ran suddenly out of the craft and back to the house, vaulting majestically over the ever-increasing piles of Bellsurpians lying recumbent at his feet.

"Sir," he hollered as he burst through the door to find Swamsoot almost purple and rubbing his buttocks between each minor elevation. "It's the right planet, but the language decipherer seems to think there may be some cross-over areas where the terminology may be ambiguous, so to speak."

"Ambiguous?" Swamsoot responded with a hint of anger for the first time. "Why didn't it tell us that on the way here?"

"Because it's a machine, sir."

"And why didn't it tell us there may be some areas of confusion to distract us from the original plan?"

"Because it's a machine, sir."

Swamsoot shook his head. "Stop repeating yourself, Delius."

"Certainly, sir."

"And find out the answer to those questions. Otherwise, we might have to retreat to a safer haven to observe the more subtle characteristics of the inhabitants."

"Right away, sir," Delius answered without asperity and, once again, disappeared out of the house and off in the direction of the ship. Captain Swamsoot began the process of regaining his composure, although he wished for the gift of being able to blow on his own buttocks. This, in turn, sent reasonable vibes to the now frantic Calistones and other counterparts, who now formed piles so high that Tam was beside himself with mirth to the extent he felt like joining them in a pile-on. One thing Tam Wilson was not, however, was a man to be seen enjoying himself. At least not by the locals.

"Fancy a roll on the floor with your mates?" asked the considerably perkier Scot, who, in turning his anguish to good nature, presented a far prettier picture to Swamsoot. "If you're not frightened of your own shadow, that is?" he continued, almost breaking into a goad mode. Sadly, this served to do nothing other than bring the confusion pangs flooding back with a vengeance.

Those Calistones who had picked up on the skipper's freshening thoughts were thrown into a calamitous hubbub as they stumbled wildly from one thorny bush to the next. Naturally, their reliant colleagues doubled their efforts and found themselves falling like trees in the forest of Dutch Elm Disease. Having followed instructions to return to the ship for more information, Delius was horrified to look out of the viewing panel to see the mounds of flesh stacking up again like an allotment owner's autumn manure heap.

"All hands to rescue pods," he shouted at the P.A system before realising it was switched off. One try later, all hands did make themselves available and filled up the pods as instructed. "Seek all colleagues, including Captain Swamsoot and return here with all haste."

Like the excited teenagers that they were like, they released the pods onto the ground below them and began clearing up the carnage caused by the crazy confusion. In the biggest of the piles of people lay groaning masses of men and Calistones, all ready for their beds after supper and a hefty helping of pudding. Some were crying for their Mothers whilst a number of them complained of crab apple belly in an attempt to initiate some level of sympathy for their bruised and battered bones. Meanwhile, Swamsoot looked hard and long at Tam, who stood spellbound by the window, astonished by the front garden activity.

"Do your parents know where you all are?" asked the pensive Scot, his hangover dissipating with every weird happening.

"Almost certainly and they'll be very disappointed if we don't sell you some of these little snippets here," answered Swamsoot, pointing to an empty table. Tam also looked, but by comparison, pointing to a table full of nothing compared to the scene from Braveheart on his lawn was minuscule. Seconds later, the front door burst open and a party of travelling Bellsurpians ran in to take back their captain with all the stealth of a constipated rhino making its first movement for three weeks.

"What now?" Tam enquired rationally.

"Don't worry," Swamsoot reassured him. "They're crazy. Leave me alone," he hollered at the press gang trying to force him through the door.

"Never," answered the unruly mob as they ushered him back towards the craft at shoulder height, happy that they had saved the most important man on the mission and each of them beginning to dream about medals on chests and statues on mantelpieces. It was at times such as these that Swamsoot yearned for wiser, more proficient crew members but knew in his heart that this was as good as it would get. It seemed pointless struggling and his lasting memory would be Tam's face as they dragged him back to the craft where he would waste two days explaining that he was in no danger to a team of dis-believers. Beyond the frustrations he was experiencing, though, lay a real breakthrough in that Tam's experience had shocked him so much that he decided to stop drinking. When next they landed in his garden, Tam Wilson would be sober for the first time in fifteen years.

Being of sound mind and body, Damalgo Winstonian Swamsoot was almost unique in terms of Bellsurpians. His ability to speak whilst in an upright position meant he was always destined for bigger and better things than most of his friends, which in turn meant he lost a lot of friends.

Dark, sunken eyes made him a hit with the opposite sex, but a refusal to cry at the sight of a bee made him too hard to make a worthwhile gamble for any would-be Bellsurpian bride.

His short, cropped military-style hair identified him as one of the good types, as Bellsurp's regimental regime was held in great esteem by their neighbours, as well as their enemies. Advanced civilisations such as this no longer fought wars, the common-sense approach having reached their part of the universe some thousands of years beforehand, meaning all military purpose was to improve life, as opposed to diminishing it. Although civilisations in the same sector still fought battles, any armoury had been long since removed and most of the battles were fought with fists or the vicious tongues of the most feared adversaries in the universe. The Sarcasticaries.

These men and women had perfected a fighting tool that could cut a man down from thousands of miles away and each and every Bellsurpian government was criticised for developing such a monstrous craft by not removing their 'dry wit' gene before setting them free on these rogue planets. Swamsoot had long since been a supporter of the 'cut them free' movement, which set out its life's work by detailing how it would educate The Sarcasticaries to understand that people's feelings could be hurt. Sadly, The Sarcasticaries had developed their own way of dealing with things and had gone underground in an attempt to fend off any would-be changers. Camps were set up in Bellsurpian deserts and initiation ceremonies took place to conscript potential cheeky sorts. As soon as they were able to verbally disrespect someone, they could expect to be shipped to one of the rogue planets where insults would be sent via all manner of communication, including the danatronical starflash, otherwise known as the intergalactic internet.

On one such message, did the purpose of Swamsoot's mission come to light when a small craft was identified by space watchers and a message was received from The Sarcasticaries condemning its very existence? Trust being in such short supply between the two factions. The Bellsurpians assumed it was sent by The Sarcasticaries and they, in return, believed it to be a Bellsurpian spy ship.

'Oh yes. Nice ship!' The Sarcasticaries posted on the danatronical starflash for all Bellsurpian computer geeks to see. The message noted an exploratory flight took off to see what the hubbub was about and why these mocking outcasts would send such a caustic message; so caustic indeed that it had included an exclamation mark. An urgent summary was passed back to HQ stating a craft had been found with a picture of a man and a woman daubed on the side and further investigations showed a crude level of intelligence had sent the machine into the stratosphere. Clearly, The Sarcasticaries couldn't have mustered enough of the base materials to undertake such a task and so, a search of the airwaves was ordered from on high.

Radio signals were intercepted from the general direction of the uncomplicated craft and amongst the messages was an array of bizarre, condescending demands on the recipient, whomsoever that may have been. Flustered and confused by these propositions, the rulers of Bellsurp commissioned a report to be compiled to identify what manner of creature could be so brutal as to tell its people it would win a fortune by 'simply opening this letter' or 'by ringing this number'.

While a host of individuals assumed the whole gamut was an ill-conceived joke perpetrated by troublemakers, others watched and waited with a nervous yearning for information, hopeful that a sensible answer would be forthcoming. What they didn't expect was a civilisation apparently controlled by these quirks known as 'advertising' and that the whole of the civilised part of this civilisation depended on this advertising for their needs.

Incredibly, adverts formed a junket into fantasy for the inhabitants of the strange planet and without them, the race didn't know how to function or progress. Millions of the inhabitants did survive without the adverts, but for no obvious reason, they did not possess what the advertees owned.

Comfort.

Soon after the initial ship passed by the planet, a collection of information was compiled for the academics to deduce whatever could be deduced and the government officials were invited to hear the outcomes, along with the military top brass. Here, Swamsoot not only made a name for himself but also became the first military man for as long as anyone could remember, brave enough to speak at a public gathering. Scholastic high flyers dominated the proceedings as they tried to make sense of the information that almost slipped past their planet in the dead of night.

Most other evenings, the sky watchers would have been dozing merrily in their hideaways while the darkness did its dirty work and kept cowards locked up tight. Anything other than light was not acceptable to a race who feared fear itself and, worse than that, the dark. However, on a night when Boris Whitehall watched from his observatory for confirmation, or otherwise, of flying fairies, he picked up on the craft, moving at a terminally slow pace in the alley to the Z-sector of Bellsurp. All relevant agencies were notified and the craft was duly intercepted, whereupon the basic information it carried and sought was extracted. Boris was given a congressional medal for being brave enough to look outside when it was dark and everyone else set about trying to get to the bottom of the craft and its message.

On any other day, the military top brass may well have been at the cinema, but as the seminar was called on a day with a 'P' in it, they agreed to attend, provided the buffet was suitable and plentiful.

As was the case with these functions, it started with an oath of allegiance; 'What do we love?' shouted the master of ceremonies.

'Bellsurp' answered the masses and the seminar began in earnest. Ordinarily, the oath of allegiance could take up half of the day with pledges of unmitigated support for sausages, fluffy toys and squares with round corners, but the general feeling today was one of 'let's get on with it'. This attitude, Swamsoot believed, was what set the military apart from the multitudes that they protected with general running around and working for the greater good. In the past, the military had been utilised only as a fighting force, but since the softiness had taken hold, nobody would sign up for an organisation that promoted violence. Thankfully, everyone had seen the benefits of production as opposed to destruction and the armies of Bellsurp were now looked up to with a feeling of awe and veneration. Lest anyone forget, however, pictures of the 'Great Bashing of the King's Soldiers' hung in the reception of every army base, where people were invited to talk about careers in the forces and eat chocolate biscuits. It was a good life.

As was the way with these get-togethers, the most boring person was given the task of sending everyone to sleep with a little slice of nothing. Albert Fatfield was not about to let anyone down and within minutes of commencement, a dozen or so had nodded off and most of the remainder furtively read books and comics.

"… and in conclusion," he said with the first bit of feeling in an hour-long speech. "I would like to wish you all a Merry Dortifloor and enjoy the rest of the seminar." Books slammed shut, comics were folded away and the absentees re-entered the hall where the real speakers were clambering onto the platform to debate the interception of the primitive craft and the messages it carried. Speakers such as the next batch made seminars bearable, as words were seen as an unnecessary waste of time and energy.

"Let's get it sorted." Colonel Wilti suggested and returned to his seat to a huge, warm ovation.

General Battleprop was every bit as ebullient. "We need to let the clever people sort this out." And the whole day from that moment followed a trend whereby anyone on his or her feet for more than ten seconds was slow-hand-clapped or deemed to be a scientist.

Being a scientist on a day like this, however, was being in the right place at the right time because the Bellsurpian scientists would make a mark on this day in history, which would ultimately be classed as indelible. Lacklustre speeches from the militia were almost to be expected, but the scientists it was who identified a whole host of oddments from the next Galaxy but one, meaning intelligent life forms, were abusing the right to hold the title.

It wasn't the first time, of course, as many years earlier, another planet vaguely decreed parity to the 'intelligent life' banner was also investigated and eventually had the title revoked when it was found to be harbouring fugitives from a 'bad place'. Although 'bad places' were a tad subjective in their descriptions, once a decision was taken on Bellsurp, it never faced opposition. Two-party politics was summarily dismissed as too complicated and the whole nation spoke as one and this seminar would not go anywhere near breaking that tradition.

In a green room in a street that nobody visited, two of General Battlerprop's supporters sat in front of their respective computers, figuring out exactly how far they could fire a missile.

"Quite far," one of them said. "That should be enough."

Only one man knew they were there.

Stumble Across the Best Made Plans

"It appears to me," Doctor Willipoop addressed the gathering. "That for a planet to control its subjects with such drivel is either the mark of pompous lunatics or complete men of great propensity." A muttering of agitation rolled out across the room. "Clever people." It was all so simple when spoken in simple terms. "Should these people be as clever as they *might* be, they could be a threat to the whole of creation, mainly because they have weapons bigger than pea shooters."

"Bigger than pea shooters?" screamed a voice from the crowd, horrified by the very notion of someone wanting to kill a pea.

"We need to investigate further," Willipoop continued as the pea lover was escorted from the auditorium. "We need to either embrace them or destroy their willpower."

"Never!" screamed a voice from the rear, but that was allowed to slide into the background when the crowd realised it was a refusal to buy a quasi-religious comic to help fund a place for homeless drunken sailors. Everyone else wholly agreed with the good doctor and the consensus was consummated in that no detail had been discussed, but everyone trusted the scientists. Therefore, the detail didn't really matter. It did have to be discussed to a degree, though, so the debate began in earnest immediately after the cream cakes and juice.

Doctor Willipoop wiped the cream off his top lip and re-addressed his captive audience with a haunting proclamation. "If we allow these people to continue without at least confronting their barbaric actions, we may be leaving ourselves open to attack in future times and an end to all we love." A few rumblings could be heard, but most of it was digestive sounds. "Unless we can go and actually determine 'why' they behave the way they do, we will be shooting in the dark."

Words such as 'shooting' and 'dark' were scary enough for most Bellsurpians to turn and run, but the military men were in the room and everyone in this space sector knew how brave the military men were. That many didn't notice ten of the military men running home crying at the mention of the two fearsome words was unimportant and the meeting continued with the seats pushed closer together.

"We appear to have intercepted a series of messages whereby the leaders of this nation tell the subordinates exactly what they should be spending their currency on and that they will be in trouble if they don't heed the warnings." A myriad of exclamations whooshed up from the crowd and the good doctor knew he had hit a nerve. "More importantly though, is that many of these subjects feel so terrified that they rush out and spend their feeble resources on what can only be described as 'pap'. And some of them end up ruing the day they ever heeded the notification to spend the last of the family savings, but once it's gone…" Willipoop threw up his arms, confident he didn't have to complete the tale and most of the assembly tutted at the horror of being forced to spend. Additionally, however, a high number deduced the good doctor's microphone had stopped working and were frantically asking neighbours how he finished the sentence. Suddenly, amidst the general hubbub that followed the dramatic maxim with which the doctor had left them hanging, a voice called out from the throng before him.

"So, should we invade them?" cried a shrill squawk with the type of positive tone to suggest he was an arms dealer.

"It's abominable!" exclaimed another and for a moment, the meeting looked as though it would spiral out of control.

"Gentlemen, please," General Battleprop interceded, ambling to the stage with lukewarm zest. "I don't like the sound of what I'm hearing any more than you do, but we need to let the clever people give us all of the details. Then we'll invade them." Once more, he received a bone-shaking ovation as he trundled back to his seat, having pocketed one of the doctor's sweeties from the podium. Willipoop coughed politely and then proceeded to outline the plans as drawn up by his team of top thinkers. They included Benjamin Daisy, who had become the youngest pharmacist to the throne at the tender age of ninety-four and although he was constantly reminded, he tried to overlook his 'way' with the opposite sex.

The Daisyman, as nicknamed, was an absolute whiz with the Bellsurpian women and but for his dalliances with a number of married sorts, he could have been aiming for a spot on the politician's podium. Naturally, this was a dream he refused to give up on and he continued to try and upgrade his affair numbers until he succeeded. Daisyman was also popular with the men, although his popularity on that front stemmed from a strong sense of purpose when batting at the crease. Crease batting was a national sport involving a bat and a crease and, where appropriate, a pair of light-coloured trousers. Most Bellsurpian women hated crease batting, but Daisy Man was everything every male Bellsurpian wanted to be in sport; a real man's man.

For the business at hand, however, he was also a bit of a smart-arse and Willipoop could not have made the level of progress without him and his stature within the professional community. A purr of expectation filled the room when Benjamin Daisy climbed to his feet to address the mob.

"All right then?" he asked politely before rushing headlong into his theory. "It is my considered opinion that these creatures have a little too much intelligence to simply wipe them out but insufficient intelligence to defy our superior control techniques. Should we have to arrive at a confrontational position…" Six people ran out of the room. "Then we have the technology to ply their fluid supplies with Deerdroppinall, thus rendering them completely susceptible to our ideals and wishes. Although this won't constitute a formal take-over of a planet, it is the next best thing and we can even leave flags there if we want to." Hordes of hands sprouted vivaciously skyward while muffled, audible crowing resembling 'me, me' could be almost heard. "Does anyone have a question that isn't 'what's Deerdroppinall?" Before he could scratch his posterior, the efflorescence of waving hands had vanished and the muttering had disappeared entirely from earshot. "I see. In that case, allow me to elucidate." Just before the hands returned to block out the skyline, he started again. "Allow me to explain.

Deerdroppinall is a sweet-flavoured liquid that has an attraction to all known creatures and leaves anyone who consumes it at the power and disposal of anyone who happens to be within persuasion distance. It is informally known as the 'disaffection fixer' or, as we scientists like to call it, 'the drug that allows people with the inclination the ability to completely indoctrinate individuals with any type of mindset we so choose'. Catchy, isn't it?"

And catchy it was, proving without any question that the clever people were indeed the right people to deal with the problem at hand, meaning the only outstanding piece of business was choosing who would make the journey. A host of suitors made their arguments whilst the generals mused over the pros and cons. A young, keen Damalgo Winstonian Swamsoot sat patiently, enthralled by the heady debate and shocked by the incompetence of it all. But for his well-mannered makeup, he may well have found himself hollering directions and instructions to his colleagues surrounding him.

In the event he followed that intuitive posit, he might have been banished from the meeting place and missed the opportunity to make a name for himself as the Bellsurpian who wasn't afraid to go out into the dark sky, otherwise known as space. If, however, he had chosen to speak out and effectively disenfranchise himself, he would not have been given a crew of lunatics and Calistones, a poison chalice in anyone's books. As the discussion raged on, Swamsoot gently prodded his best friend, Bamber Wetbot and asked him what his initial thoughts were on the whole process that was unfolding before their eyes.

"Oh, I don't know Damalgo, but it seems to me this is going to take a pretty special sort of a soldier to take this on. A mad soldier, if you will."

"Mad? Why mad, Bamber?"

"Oh well, I believe that anything beyond the sky is twice as nasty as anything beneath it and almost everything you encounter smells of wee."

"Really?"

"I believe so," Bamber replied with a touch of disingenuous bravado. "And if you touch anything, you will turn into whatever it is you touch and eventually expand until you either float away or burst."

Swamsoot raised his favourite eyebrow. The left one. "Where did you hear this, exactly?"

"Oh, it's just what they say," Bamber answered without the merest hint of invention and with a smile that endeared him to most people.

"It's just what *they* say? Who are they?"

"Just the people who know, but anyway," he interjected and subsequently took all confrontation out of the discussion. "I just overheard one of the clever people say that any soldier who agrees to take on the mission will almost certainly be given a seat in the Royal palace."

"But nobody knows what the mission is yet," Swamsoot retorted, displaying a mix of impatience and hope.

"Well, I'm sure we'll get to find out today unless the generals want to spend tonight in swanky hostelries, chomping their way through horse meat and cold butter." Sharing a smile, the two friends sat back and thought about a Bellsurpian delicacy that generals and Royals could only afford and wondered how terrified the general's horses must be every day. Up on the podium, a number of generals and clever people shared a huddle, obviously deciding something very important. After a while, one of the clever people took the bull by the horns and delivered a key point to the anxious assembly.

"We all agree to remove this bull from the stage. Secondly, we all agree that we should have hot cakes and fizzy drinks for all."

A roar of unity rattled throughout the roof void and the meeting was adjourned to scoff their way through the various delights on the tables at the back of the hall. Swamsoot felt somewhat puzzled as to why so many military personnel were in attendance and decided to engage one of the clever people in conversation. At the end of the food tables stood a tall, rangy-looking clever person with a pair of spectacles and a long, white coat, compulsory items for the clever fraternity.

"Hello there," he opened casually. "My name's Swamsoot. Damalgo Swamsoot of the flying fifteenth."

"Oh, hello," she answered softly. "I'm Ethel Balldytireskid from the office of Nurexility." This *was* impressive. The office of Nurexility was viewed as the single most important office in the whole of the clever people bastion and Ethel was also very attractive.

"Nurexility, eh? Isn't that where the experiments are being carried out to determine the viability of telling lies and getting away with it?"

"Yes, the Government is very keen to see the use of telling lies and a lot of our guinea pigs are the politicians themselves. Naturals."

"Really?" asked the young man in his nineties. "So, do you know why so many of my colleagues are here today?"

"Oh yes. I think it's because they've been invited."

"No, I mean, why so many military people, as opposed to, say… farmers?"

"Why would the farmers be invited to deal with the invasion of another planet?" asked the attractive young, clever person.

"Invasion? Who said anything about an invasion?" Swamsoot's voice had managed to peak at about the level a dolphin would understand and the clever person was clearly impressed with his pitch.

"Ooh!" she said submissively. "I like a man who can crack glass with his delivery of an emotion. Perhaps you and I can go for a cup of hot bontap sauce sometime?" As much as he loved the juice of the local bontap, Swamsoot was now distracted by the notion of all-out invasion. All-out invasion meant all-out war and Bellsurpians were not prepared for war, nor would they ever be.

Most of his fellow Bellsurpians were too frightened to talk about war in history class due to so much of the fighting having been carried out in the dark. Even some of his military contemporaries were afraid of anyone's shadow, including their own and wouldn't set foot outside of their barracks if civil unrest was on the television. Civil Unrest was, in fairness, the most popular game show on television and soldiers often tried to take part in the format by ringing the number on the screen and telling the populous how they would defend the cake shops if the milk was two hours late. Other scenarios included military personnel explaining how they would deal with a draft board and the obvious solutions such as 'buy a draft excluder' were deemed to be Bellsurpian classics and nobody passed the opportunity to use old well-worked puns.

"Why would they want to invade someone?" asked the increasingly unnerved young man of the increasingly attractive young scientist. "It's not in our make-up to go invading other planets, especially planets that we don't know anything about."

Ethel suddenly became noticeably evasive. "Shall we go and see if there are any of the sweet shells left from the cake mixture?" she asked with a glimmer of a blush crossing her cheeks like a teenager's first experience of classroom flatulence. Swamsoot's manners were, as ever, impeccable, but he would not be put off the scent.

"OK then. I love those sweet shells and perhaps you can tell me why we're going to invade a strange planet while we're there?" He smiled the sort of smile to melt a witch's heart and Ethel Balldytireskid fell under his charm spell.

Women the length and breadth of Bellsurp swooned as the military wandered past with swords gleaming in the bright light that lit up their skies. That the swords were made from a sponge material made the appearance even more tempting for those women who dared to approach the warriors who stoutly defended their planet from name-callers. During his service, Swamsoot had racked up a number of would-be conquests but managed to maintain his integrity by being terrified of women. Ethel, though, for no obvious reason, seemed to be a little different. *Perhaps,* he thought, *it was down to her being gorgeous, as opposed to the monsters by whom he had been pursued over his career in the armed forces. This woman might just be the one...* "You're not thinking of taking a life partner, are you?" he asked without thinking.

Not un-typically, Ethel was as impressed as a father is on catching his daughter climbing out of the window with a politician holding the eloping ladder. "What a ridiculous question!" And in an instant, he had fallen head over heels for a woman he had known for a couple of minutes.

"How nice of you to say," he answered without hearing her words. "Do you think it's a good idea to invade this planet then?"

"This planet? Who's going to invade this planet?" The anxiety in her voice shook sense into the normally unflappable Swamsoot and he reversed into common sense gear, a position he was widely known for.

"I don't mean *this* planet, Ethel. I mean this planet that we're talking about. Whatever it's called."

"Oh, well, in that case, yes, I do." In the confusion, Swamsoot was temporarily baffled, as her answer was a well-known retort to another well-known question.

"You do what? I only seek clarification as I appear to have asked two disparate questions in a short space of time and I'm not absolutely sure which of them you're answering." As if speaking to a child, she tipped her head kindly to one side and spoke more slowly than was polite.

"Why don't you ask me the questions again and I'll try not to use so many long words?" It was at best patronising and at worst downright rude to the extent of requiring satisfaction by way of a duel, but he was a Bellsurpian after all and duels weren't for cowards. Nonetheless, as the woman he was prepared to do anything for, having submitted his love gene some minutes ago, he smiled at her sweetly enough to produce bile from onlookers.

"As you wish, Ethel." And he did indeed repeat the questions and she answered the same way as before and the remainder of their time together was an absolute joy. Only the seriousness of the seminar prevented them from wandering off aimlessly like a pair of slack-jawed teenage simpletons to proffer to one another their undying love. As it happened, the seminar became boisterous and ill-tempered, meaning the opportunity for them to spend more time together never materialised and Swamsoot discovered a side to himself that he was unaware of. As a plethora of clever people spoke on the platform, followed by not-so-clever military men, Swamsoot found himself being drawn into a heated debate about which he had no real knowledge. General Battleprop spoke clearly and concisely about his army's plans and how they would be carried out to the letter.

It went without saying that nobody except the clever people would question the general.

"The problem is," started the old war-horse. "We can't take a chance on leaving a race with so little in the way of intellect with as much destructive capacity. Goodness knows what they might engineer for any neighbours or, indeed, for their own ecosystems. It's quite clear to my team and me that the only solution is to take them out of the game and move on before any damage is done." Benjamin Daisy saw a much more inventive prospect in this exercise.

"With respect to the general and his dim team, we have much too good an opportunity to experiment with this race and gain invaluable lessons from whatever it is they appear to have developed into. The worst thing we could do is to simply wipe them out just because they're not terribly bright."

"Not terribly bright?" the belligerent general hollered. "They're bright enough to have created weapons that could wipe out nations and they have people running their countries who don't know how to fly." The irony wasn't lost on anyone. "They are a complete waste of a planet and should be treated as such." Across the room, Swamsoot could see the lovely Ethel becoming agitated at her colleagues' inability to articulate what most of the clever people thought and she had witnessed with these situations before where the soldiers always won.

Such frustrations, however, were a part of a clever person's life and she was accustomed to the disappointments. Swamsoot caught her eye and flashed a smile, which she returned without too much enthusiasm. *I must speak out on her behalf,* he thought, although he didn't have the first idea as to what she was thinking or wanted, so he sat in silence as the discussion raged on. Even Bamber Wetbot chose to bolster the soldier's cause by underlining the general's position.

"I have a family to think about on Bellsurp and I can't afford to let these mischievous morons run a planet on not enough brain power to get a shuttle craft off the ground, circle the planet sixty times and arrive back in time for late supper." As was the way with these occasions, Bamber received a standing ovation from the military attendees whilst the clever people shouted for his resignation. And amongst it all, Swamsoot was finding it increasingly difficult to concentrate on anything other than the lovely Ethel, whose face looked as miserable as a horse facing a two-mile uphill trek with a milk cart at its back. He would do anything to alleviate her suffering and just then, Melchione Madder entered the room to whisper something to his boss.

"Captain Swamsoot," he murmured with standard Calistone uncertainty. "I've found the buttons off your pyjamas, sir. They were underneath your bed, behind the pictures you had downloaded from the starflash of…"

"All right, Madder, that's enough information. But…" Naturally, being a Calistone, Madder knew what he wanted before he asked but felt an explanation was in order as it seemed a tad peculiar.

"You want me to read General Battleprop's mind and see what he 'really' wants?"

"What? No, no, you're looking at the wrong person on the podium." And indeed, Madder's crossed eyes could only focus on what he thought he was being directed to, the elderly pompous general at the front of the room.

"I'm pleased it's not him you want me to mind-read because I've read his thoughts before and…"

"Madder!" Swamsoot whispered with just enough restraint to stop his spittle from covering everyone in the immediate vicinity. "You know you aren't allowed to read minds without permission of a better or an almost reasonable."

"Sorry, sir," Madder answered, dropping his shameful eyes to the floor. "Do you want me to read someone else's mind?"

"I should jolly well think you are sorry," admonished Swamsoot with a half-hidden titter in his voice. "I want you to read the mind of the young woman to the right of the general at the rear of the podium, about fifteen degrees northwest of his seat." Madder paused between involuntary movements of his quivering lips. "The woman with the red shirt on, Madder."

"Yes, sir, sir." There followed a short hiatus before Madder returned his gaze to Swamsoot, who sat spellbound in anticipation. "It appears she wants someone to take a crew to the stupid planet and do a few tests before they blow it up. Additionally, sir, it appears she would do anything to have one of these empty-headed military sorts chew without displaying his tonsils, sir."

"I see. What about…"

"Also, sir, it would seem she also thinks that the only reason that the military exists is to make sure the bright people never run out of food, mainly because they would make reasonable sandwiches out of their thick heads, sir."

"So does she…"

"And, sir, she is suggesting…"

"All right, Madder. I think I understand her point now, so you can."

"Actually, sir, there's lots more I haven't touched on yet."

"Another day, Madder, another day." Swamsoot stood up meaningfully and waved to catch the eye of the speaker at the front of the hall. Inevitably, the walk forward was greeted by the military as another spokesman for the good cause and the clever people winced with expectation of another puerile attempt to stir up the military masses into an eating frenzy. When he reached the stage, his gaze across the crowded floor was returned by soldiers grinning like drunken idiots, peppered with waves likened to parents encouraging their children at the Christmas play.

A feeling of stolid guilt suddenly hit him and he wondered if the emotion compelling him to desert in the face of the clever people would result in his disenfranchisement. Or worse, the removal of the company fertiliser discount card. Regardless, however, he strode manfully to the microphone when it was his turn and opened with a cough. Even under such circumstances, Swamsoot was a little taken aback by the ovation he received for clearing his throat.

Nonetheless, he remained cool in adversity and waited for the clapping to stop before he began.

"Captain Damalgo Winstonian Swamsoot, from the Battalion of Royal Guards of Secret Personages of Bellsurp and the Leader of the Movement to Support the Right to Shake Hands in any Fashion." After the initial ovation, he half expected another for the introduction and simply stepped back to allow the noise to dissipate before carrying on with his address. "I believe the simplest route through this would be to send a landing party to this hideous planet of no-hopers and at least try and ascertain what it is that makes them as dumb as they seem. If that's unsuccessful, at least we will have learnt some valuable information about civilisation and perhaps we can prevent it from happening again elsewhere."

As he marched back towards his seat, the deafening silence was making him feel nauseous, but the lack of foot stamping and baying for blood was strangely comforting to him. Ethel lowered her head and smiled like a teenage girl and he looked up to Madder when he arrived back at his seat, who confirmed exactly what he wanted to hear.

"She's delighted, sir and yes, she does want to engage in some form of physical activity to the degree of…"

"Thank you, Madder. That will be all for now, but you might want to hang around outside in case I need you later for…"

"Yes, sir." And Madder knew what he meant because it was his job to know. Still, though, the silence was horrendous and only when General Battleprop clambered to his feet did the mood change.

"Just what I was saying," he proclaimed with delight and raised a pointed finger at Swamsoot menacingly. "But I'm happy to say that our up-and-coming youngsters say these things much better than the old guard like me and my like. Now how can you people," he continued with the same raised finger crucially directed towards the clever people. "Disagree with what has been said there? It makes sense to go and see what these people are made of and that way, we retain credibility as well as offering an opportunity to improve whatever meagre lifestyles they have." All around the hall, heads were coming together at such speed it seemed only a matter of time before a serious accident occurred.

Clever people saw sense in this young soldier's stance and soldiers saw sense in whatever Battleprop had apparently agreed to. If a worry still existed, it was in Swamsoot's mind in case he had said something without realising. "Let's get him back up here and give him the support he deserves." Battleprop went on, serving only to terrify Swamsoot further in the midst of his confused state. In line with the general's request, however, the room stood and applauded like never before and as he returned to the podium, he noticed the curtains were shaking to the extent he expected them to fall off. He also noticed the green and yellow striped pattern was quite vile, but to mention this would be to violate the special code of conduct and conformity that existed between the armed forces and the textile manufacturers of Bellsurp. Being a pragmatic young man, he simply chose to take a polite bow without mentioning the curtains. Being a snitch, Madder would pass his thoughts on the next time he saw a curtain maker.

As he stood before the frenetic masses, who were busy whooping like a game show audience, Swamsoot turned and smiled at Ethel, who smiled back sweetly. The chemistry between them was interrupted by a chemist as Benjamin Daisy stepped forward to shake his hand and so blotted out any sight of the lovely Ethel.

"I suppose you'll be wanting all of the glory yourself, eh?" asked the tall, rangy scientist.

"Glory?"

"He most certainly will," Battleprop interrupted and threw him into total confusion and doubled up on the uncertainty levels as to what he had been talking about. "Young Swamsoot here is one of the brightest young upstarts in the universe that we believe in and possibly some of the fictitious parts as well."

"Here, here," drifted up from the crowd.

"It seems only fair to me that the spark as bright as the one to devise this plan must be the one to carry it out. Imagine how we'd feel if someone else went and didn't make the most of young Swamsoot's plan?"

"Plan?" asked Swamsoot.

"And imagine," the general shot back. "If we allowed him to go without an incentive of some description? The good people of Bellsurp would call us worse than Earthlings and rightly so."

"I agree," Benjamin Daisy noted enthusiastically. "And I think it only fair that we also devise some sort of incentive to help support the programme as well. Obviously, we don't want people thinking you birds at the military side of life are the only ones interested in saving planets."

"Incentive?" asked Swamsoot meekly.

"That's not the worst idea you've had Daisy. I've always said we should put our heads together in an attempt to better the place for us all and I'm only glad young Swamsoot here has brought us together for everyone to see what we can achieve. Harmony and accord."

"Exactly, general Battleprop. That's what we've both been missing for as long as I care to remember and young Swamsoot here has shown us the error of our ways."

"Harmony and accord?" Swamsoot was now whispering.

"Tell you what we'll do then Daisy; let's retire to our respective camps and delegate a bit of responsibility to our subordinates and get our best people involved in this think tank. What do you say?" It was much too good an offer to spurn and Benjamin Daisy offered his hand as a sign of gentlemanly conduct before turning his attention to his team and signalling the way back to their conference room. Battleprop did likewise and both men stood as though on a pedestal accepting plaudits from all corners and virtually canoodling like a pair of smitten teenagers declaring their mutual respect for one another. Within a minute, they were out of sight of each other's parties and spoke now with earnest.

"Right then," Battleprop started with venom. "I want everyone moving at the speed of light on this and make sure we get our act together before the egg-heads in the other room. We're not giving this one up for those nose-pickers."

The clever people were notorious when it came to nasal extractions, although most chose to ignore it.

"Right then," Daisy said to his team. "We need to get a jump on the empty heads over there. Their brain cells may be as lonely as a hermit on the island of anonymity, but they do have enough pull with the government to get a jump on us here if we let them. All we need to do is produce a plan with enough long words in it to confuse them."

And so the tiff went on behind closed doors and Swamsoot watched quietly as it took place, wondering what he had done, why he had done it and whether or not he would get a snog at the end of it off Ethel Balldytireskid. In the other conference room, Ethel stared at Benjamin Daisy, wondering if he was speaking any sense at all or whether or not her emotions had been stirred by a young military man who had taken the time out to try and impress her. During her young life to date, no man had taken any notice of her at all, mainly because she was officially a genius and terrified most people with her brilliance. Swamsoot was bright enough but wasn't fazed by her obvious genius and smart way of thinking. Somewhere in the plan, which was to be unfolded, they would meet again, and hopefully, for them both, they would be allowed some time to get to know each other properly and if that included a snog, then so be it.

When Great Minds Collide

It seemed as though everyone had conspired against him and Swamsoot was never taken to moments of paranoia, so he assumed that everyone *had* indeed conspired against him.

"Could you explain it to me once more, please?" he asked the equally grumpy collective of General Battleprop and Benjamin Daisy.

"After you," Battleprop offered to his counterpart, who was clearly as upset as the mighty military man.

"Oh no. After you, my good man, after all, we wouldn't want one of your men travelling across the galaxy with an order to either educate or destroy a planet and you not giving him the instruction." Battleprop stared carefully at Daisy, then at the wide-eyed Swamsoot.

"The thing is Swamsoot, we intend to send a party of your choice to this planet Earth and with a bit of luck, you'll come back with the news that they've mended their ways and are indeed capable of reasonable existence."

"And what if they aren't?"

"Kill them all!" interrupted Daisy quite uncharacteristically.

"Kill them all?" Swamsoot asked with a voice high enough to crack the royal crystal. There immediately followed a message via one of the Calistone guards to lower the voice pitch by order of the King's Cutlery and Fancy Goods Manager. "I can't go killing a civilisation." It was a point well made, but in the main, overlooked.

"Listen to me Swamsoot," started Battleprop with his most menacing of looks on his face. "As you suggested this whole damn charade in the first place, it's only fair that you undertake the task at hand. Unless," he shouted with a squealed interruption. "You'd rather pass it to the good doctor here and his cohorts?"

"Well, actually," started the inexperienced soldier, but recognised the anger on the face of the boss. "It will probably be a good experience for me and my… Did you say a crew of my choice?"

"What I say and what I mean are two entirely different things."

"You do get a say in the party, Swamsoot," Daisy explained softly. "But the King has agreed that this has to be a trip of some value to the progression of certain parts of our community."

"I see," Swamsoot answered with a lie.

"So, where we would normally send soldiers." Battleprop huffed and puffed about the room as he spoke. "We now have to send a load of idiots and do-gooders. And you, of course."

"I see!" he repeated and perpetuated the lie, but now with shock in his voice sufficient to alert his superiors.

"Does that present you with a problem?" Daisy asked earnestly.

"I don't think so, but I'm not absolutely sure who you are talking about when you say 'certain parts of the community' have to be accommodated."

"I didn't say that," Battleprop shouted.

"No, you didn't, sir, but Doctor Daisy alluded to it."

"What's that got to do with me?"

"And I'd rather not be referred to as doctor."

"And that's a doctor saying that." Battleprop reminded him, thus allowing Daisy an opportunity.

"Although if I say so, it sounds more regal coming from a more senior individual. No offence Swamsoot."

"None taken, sir."

"So if there's no offence, then our business here is concluded," Battleprop added with an air of certainty and they moved towards the door with haste.

"Excuse me, sirs. Shouldn't someone be briefing me about the mission?"

"He's a wise young man, Battleprop. You were right to let him do it instead of that other lunatic who volunteered. What was his name?"

And the door swung shut just as Battleprop was about to reply and Swamsoot sat alone in the room, not knowing what, who, where or why the trip was happening. In addition to all that had happened before, he now contemplated what type of crew would be thrust upon him. So many miles into the dark, distant space and so many years in advance of their Earthling peers meant Bellsurpians were always politically correct, which inevitably meant a number of the crew would be officially undesirables. An icy chill slipped down his back at the prospect. Try as he might, he couldn't concentrate his mind on anything other than a crew of his choice, meaning a crew he would have no say in. And he couldn't stop thinking about Ethel Balldytireskid. Within moments of the thought, Melchione Madder opened the door and made, under the circumstances, a reasonable suggestion.

"Would you like me to contact Miss Balldytireskid, sir?"

"Madder! Have you been reading my mind without permission?"

Madder paused before answering. "You don't have any Calistone blood, do you, sir?"

"No, of course not."

"Well, in that case, no, I haven't been reading your mind, sir. Shall I contact her then?"

Slightly compromised, Swamsoot conceded the position. "Yes. Ask her if she could come and…"

"Explain the mission in finite detail, sir?"

"Stop reading my mind."

"Yes, sir," Madder answered and turned to leave the room, whispering to himself. "I knew you were going to shout at me there," Swamsoot began tidying up the room and hiding undesirable parts of his male bastion under cushions in preparation for the lovely Ethel's arrival.

Looking up at the mirror above his most comfortable seat, he noticed a small blemish on his face and leant closer to get a better look. A very small mark had appeared underneath his left eye, resembling a minor abrasion to the knee or toe, usually acquired during a game of football. Swamsoot was instantly intrigued by its appearance. It seemed the obvious thing to do, so he poked it gently with a small steel needle, inducing great pain and the need to cry out in agony.

"I see," he said out loud to himself without the slightest hint of embarrassment or regret. Suddenly the blemish had taken on another different, more notable configuration. 'Perhaps I didn't poke it hard enough,' he thought and promptly poked it again, but with more vigour and violence, again inducing torrid cries and immediate reverse action from the mirror. "How strange," he said and continued to repeat the procedure until Ethel turncd up to discover Swamsoot with a mark the size of an apple on his cheek.

"Oh," she barely managed to articulate and began thinking of excuses to leave.

"Ethel. How nice of you to come and discuss the mission with me. Hopefully, you can give me the details that our so-called superiors seem unhappy to share?"

"Are you unwell?" she asked reasonably. "If it's an allergic reaction, I'm sure we can find someone without the cowardly gene." Swamsoot baulked at the thought, forgetful of the symptoms of cowardice on Bellsurp being red blotches.

"Someone else? Why would you want to find someone else to do my job?"

"I didn't say I wanted to, but if you feel as though you're not up to it, then I can make the necessary…"

"Oh," he interrupted as the light of realisation came on. "The blotch? It just appeared after I looked in the mirror and then poked away for a while with a needle to see if I could remove it. Nothing to do with the cowardice gene, you understand." Ethel seemed uncertain and questioned him further, sound in the knowledge that a cry-baby couldn't possibly lead such a mission as this pioneering trip.

"So what do you do when the lights go out?" she quizzed him without tact.

"I usually go to bed."

"And what about when the scary men from Halterneck town are making scary noises outside of your window?"

"I close the windows," Swamsoot replied confidently.

"And what would you do if you had no lights at all and no windows in your house."

Swamsoot thought only for a second before answering. "I'd walk into things."

"Right then," she said, content that he was still a hero. "Let's get down to business, shall we?"

"Can I offer you a glass of…"

"No," she stopped him with an accompanying wave of the hand. "We have too much to discuss before we consider any pleasantries. Do you understand the significance of this trip, Captain Swamsoot?"

"I think I do. I believe we could be extinguishing a planet if they don't fall into line with our preferred option for life. At least that's what it said on the radio earlier. That's reasonable, isn't it?" Not being cognisant of sarcasm, however, Ethel became visibly agitated and slid away from him on the long, leather sofa on which they had become ensconced. It didn't occur to him that his favourite planet to watch was not as popular with other Bellsurpians as it was with him. Sitting on his long, mustard-coloured, nineteen-seventies style, button-laden furniture only seemed normal to him. Sardonic wit was wasted and only the look on Ethel's face was the catalyst he required to educate her about the ways of the world beyond their own universe.

Over the next twelve hours, he discussed Earth humour and beauty and twentieth-century entertainment. He explained the meaning of making funny noises and how he had also passed on the wonder of such behaviour to a number of subordinates, including accidentally informing the Calistones. Major points such as swimming in the sea and throwing water on one another had Ethel perplexed but strangely comfortable. This Earth planet sounded unique to Ethel and her genuine interest was only surpassed by her interest in why Swamsoot had taken such an interest in a planet that was otherwise very un-extraordinary.

Long before the mystery probe had passed by Bellsurp's window, Swamsoot had been watching Earth from afar, having accidentally happened across them while surfing the multiverse web and clearly felt an affection. However, his ability to tell a tale had her immediately a fan of Earth and its inhabitants, so much so that they agreed to devise a deal to ensure it would remain safe even if Swamsoot was unable to achieve the goal as directed by his superiors.

As plans went, it wasn't brilliant and if anyone found out about it, they would both be accused of treason, a crime punishable by over zealous name-calling on Bellsurp. And with the plan almost completed, Ethel suddenly realised she hadn't briefed Swamsoot about the main objective of the official mission.

"It's really quite simple. Find a leader, make it swear allegiance to Bellsurp and if it doesn't, destroy the planet."

"I see."

"Oh," she continued matter-of-factly. "They have put it on a competition basis, so if they aren't pleased with your results, they'll offer it to the rest of the intergalactic pilots. They seem determined to test their weapons out, I'm afraid."

Swamsoot mused, "Not the norm for a Bellsurpian mission, is it? Being as we haven't been part of a war since our current existence began, I mean, it's not as though we usually wipe out existences because they don't conform to our rule." There was only one answer he could have accepted.

"It's politics."

"It certainly is," he said quietly. "It certainly is."

The World Looks Different Through My Eyes

Although he had forgotten what being sober felt like, Tam wasn't too displeased that he had stayed that way for a day and a half. Behaviour such as that he had witnessed on his lawn was somewhere between a bad dream and something he had actually experienced and didn't know if he had enjoyed or not. Staying sober, he felt sure, would allow him to reach a decision on which of the options it was. Thirty-six hours later, he decided it must have been his imagination and reached for a bottle of Scotch just as Swamsoot let himself in the back door.

"You must have been worried that you had missed the opportunity to buy the goods that will make your life infinitely better, you numbskull." Tam looked at Swamsoot, then at the bottle. "Of course, if you think you've suddenly become as bright as me, then let's see you demonstrate your new-found skills." Outside, a few anxious whispers could be heard as a very well-behaved mob milled around plaintively, conscious of the fact that any repeat of the behaviour scenes when last they visited would not be tolerated. Not known as a strict disciplinarian, Swamsoot had shocked his crew with the address when they arrived safely back on board the space ship and securely out of reach in the stratosphere.

"I can't believe what happened down there." He had started with, sending a stir of fear throughout the whole crew. "And I've locked the doors, so don't even think about trying to escape." As expected, two-thirds of the crew started crying, so he took the conscious decision to scold them all as quickly as possible. "When we collate all of the information and return, anyone caught panicking in the face of the enemy will be taken out at dawn and sniggered at. Do I make myself clear?" A few 'yes sirs' could be heard through the sobbing and he re-opened the doors and went to bed, happy that his 'fist of iron' rule had been upheld.

Now though, he was back in the thick of the action again with Tam and Jack, and only one of them seemed happy to see them back again. Swamsoot was genuinely amazed at the speed of the tail wagging and felt almost compelled to reach out and touch the swishing extremity, but as the status of both occupants was still unclear, he decided to err on the side of caution.

Turning his attention back to Tam, he re-commenced with the hard sell approach. "So unless your skills and intelligence have vaulted beyond reasonable assumption levels, you would be an even bigger idiot to overlook this offer, you dummy." Tam looked carefully at the bottle.

"So, it's not drink, then?"

"What?"

"Sorry, son, but I thought I might have imagined everything I saw the other day and put it down to the booze, you see?"

Swamsoot mused for a moment. "No, I'm rather afraid I have no idea what you mean."

Tam picked up the bottle. "Doesn't matter. I'm going to get drunk again anyway, especially if I'm going to imagine you when I'm sober." Although his first thoughts were to panic, Swamsoot knew the Calistones would pick up on the vibe and he couldn't afford another showing like the garden carnage or the enforced delay because of it.

"What's this drunk thing you refer to?" he asked earnestly, trying not to send mixed messages to the nearby mind readers.

"What's drunk?" Tam laughed. "I'll tell you what drunk is, sonny boy. Drunk is the start and finish of all that's good and bad. It's the meaning of life when you're drunk and the very opposite when you're not. It's the most sensible state of mind you can possibly imagine and when you come out of it, it's the most preposterous way of thinking ever devised. It's a way of seeing the most beautiful things in the world and the most revolting things at the same time, but only you will ever see it. It's how we get to forget and once we get there, we can't remember what we were trying to forget in the first place. I could talk all day about what drunk is, but don't take it from me, sonny boy, ask your dad."

"I'm not sure he could help from where he is," Swamsoot answered with a healthy dose of resolution.

"Where is he?" asked Tam.

"Up there," he answered, thrusting his thumb into the air and pointing skyward.

"Oh, I'm sorry, son. I didn't mean to… Well, anyway, it's said to be the root of all evil, so don't ever take a drop if you've any sense at all."

"How would you know that, being as you have no sense whatsoever?"

"You're a wee bit too cheeky for a young lad, aren't you?" Tam said with the merest hint of aggression, which the Calistones picked up on and moved back three steps form the doorway. "Take a tip from one who knows, sonny boy and don't be smart all of the time because people grow a bit sick and tired of it all after a while. I should know because I used to be a bit like you when I was a young boy."

"I doubt that very much, dopey. If you were anything like me, you wouldn't put up with such a low level of wontabrociousness."

"Wontawhattiness?"

"Wontabrociousness. The need to explore and better yourself and your people for the general betterment of life as we know it."

"My God, is that what they're teaching you at school these days? I thought they were still concentrating on the three Rs. In my day, every time they invented something new to teach kids, it was news all over the place because it happened so rarely, but it seems they find something new to teach you every day now. Do you still use your heads for thinking, or do you use computers for everything now?" As a question, it was asked with a smattering of sarcasm and a healthy dollop of disdain as Tam's view of the establishment had been dim since he fell out with the patent office over his lost legal case over the hydraulic lift he invented.

"Our technology plays a big part in everyday life. Doesn't yours?"

"Well, if it did, it might have won me a legal battle against a huge, faceless corporation." And with that, he unscrewed the bottle top and lifted a glass off the table in the middle of the room. Swamsoot immediately noticed the mould growth in the glass that had developed over a few days of inactivity and a few years of non-cleaning. "In fact," Tam went on. "If technology had been then what it is now, I could have been a millionaire living in a Scottish castle. Do you have any idea how difficult it was to register an invention without someone stealing your ideas?" Swamsoot was puzzled by the line of questioning.

"How could someone on this planet steal your ideas? We developed the Calistones for that very reason and you are nowhere near that level of competence."

"Well, I don't know what gallstones have to do with it, but I can guarantee that people have been stealing ideas here for many years, sonny boy and if I had been in a better position…" Tam's voice tailed off and he began pouring the whisky into the filthy glass. "Still, better to be happy and poor than miserable and rich, eh?"

"Why are you drinking out of a glass with life forms in it?" asked the intrepid space traveller.

Tam laughed. "Because I'm a single man who wouldn't know how to relate to any of the social skills that successful men acquire. In fact, I'm a monster."

Swamsoot stood up quickly and walked to the door where the Calistones had picked up on the vibe and had begun fastening their laces for a quick getaway. "Perhaps the monster is a bit too strong…" The Calistones immediately sensed how strong the monster was and took two more backward steps in unison, whilst Swamsoot felt for the edge of the door. "More of a loser than a monster, I suppose. After all, I don't want to pull myself down, do I?" Much of the bad grammar was bypassing Swamsoot and he decided to take the bull by the horns.

"Just exactly what do you want from me?"

Tam was slightly taken aback. "What do I want from you? I think you came visiting me without an invitation unless I'm very much mistaken and I'm pretty sure I'm not." He looked at the whisky and placed the glass back on the table with a hint of self-righteousness in his sneering look.

"You miss the point here, Tam. What I'm saying is that I can only help you if you want to be helped, but in order for me to help you, I have to know what you want."

Tam laughed, "And exactly what can you do for me, sonny boy?"

"Anything your limited mind can think of. Probably."

"Really? I'll tell you what then; you can stick another room on the back of the house there and decorate the bedrooms with nice summery colours, if that's not too much trouble."

"Is that all?"

"Well, while you're at it, why not wash the dog and see if you can get that car working that's stood in the garage for three years gathering rust and dust."

"All right. Anything else?"

"That should do for now, but I'll think of something else before the day's out. Don't worry. Fancy a cup of tea?"

Swamsoot mused momentarily. "Yes, I think that might be nice," he said and watched as Tam picked up the glass and took it into the kitchen, where he emptied it down the sink and rinsed it before filling the kettle. Outside, the Calistones were passing on the orders being transmitted from their illustrious leader and space travelling soldiers were scurrying back and forth to the ship to collect materials and equipment. Conscious of the activity, Jack clambered to his feet and slid out of the open door to watch the action and lay down in the early morning sunshine to watch them perform.

For a dog, it had already started as a perfect day. Tam had scratched him, fed him and walked him and now there were strangers running about so quickly he felt as though he had died and gone to a doggy heaven where cats were in such abundance that juicy ones could be caught by simply holding out a paw. Dreams like this were frequently passing through Jack's head, although he had never seen fit to pass them on to anyone. After all, who is interested in anyone else's dreams? In one of his dreams, the cats all have limps, making the chase acceptable on the basis he would never fail. In his youth, dreams were made up of cats escaping to the treetops or safely back into the arms of their stupid human owners. Being of sound mind and body, Jack tried not to dwell too much on dreams and spent his time pleasing his master. Thus, the need to chase, trip or cajole cats was almost a nightmare, let alone a pleasurable jaunt into the world of the unconscious. Jack was the happiest dog on Scroat and no other dog could make the same boast. That he was one of only five canines on the small island made the boast easy, but his competition offered nothing by way of a fight for the title of 'laughing dog of Scroat', a title he cared passionately about.

Tam shouted from the kitchen to Swamsoot and flicked on the kettle switch as he hollered. "Tea, sonny boy?"

"F," replied Swamsoot with confidence and notched another odd tradition on his space utility belt.

"Do you want a cup of tea, is what I mean, or would you prefer coffee?"

"Oh, tea, please," Swamsoot answered and rubbed his hands with glee. Most of his favourite television shows from Earth featured people drinking tea and now he was to venture into the world of show business by consuming his own. Although it seemed to take him an eternity, Tam returned with two mugs full of hot tea and placed them both on the table. "Biscuit?"

Swamsoot guessed. "Yes?"

"I only have fig rolls."

Swamsoot guessed again. "A medical condition?" Tam overlooked the crass joke and lifted the box of fig rolls out of the drawer next to his seat and offered them to the young visitor. Jack heard the rustle and decided he had been lying in the sun too long, especially as the fig rolls were his personal favourite. Stretching as he stood, he felt the ground disappear from underneath him as he was whisked lightly away to a warm tub of soapy water and washed thoroughly. Not many things bugged Jack, but washing was not what he deemed to be a natural function and in the forty-nine of his dog years he had spent with Tam, only once had he been forced to endure a wash. This, however, was not like the previous wash. This was like a gentle, warm, gratifying wash. It felt as though the hands were soft and warm and when he looked, they were even softer than he expected as they were invisible and not actually attached to anyone. Being a dog, Jack didn't dwell on the fact that he was being washed by nobody or nothing and as the invisible person washed his under-carriage, he smiled the smile of a dog that had been won over by intergalactic visitors.

"So, how long are you here for, sonny?" Tam asked, totally oblivious to his dog's pleasures outside in the sunshine.

"As long as it takes, I suppose."

"As long as it takes?" repeated the sober Scot. "As long as what takes? Are you doing some sort of project for school?"

"Similar by broad definition, although it's nothing you would understand unless you were to let me offer you some help on that front and goodness knows you need it." The comment bypassed Tam like a bullet passing an innocent bystander.

"Well, when I was at school, I did a project on a field trip about little flies that walk on water and it took me a bit of time to get it to sound as though it wasn't a religious creature." He smiled, but Swamsoot didn't. "Walking on water. Get it?"

Naturally, he didn't get it but pretended he did. "Of course," he said as he leant forward to pick up the fig rolls. "How many of these should I take, Tam, as I don't want to confuse you anymore than I have to and make the job even harder."

"Take a couple," Tam insisted and took a careful sip from the hot tea. Not being a race of hot drinkers, his guest followed suit with a big gulp.

"Great Blanderers Wampoot!" he screamed as the hot drink scalded his lips and throat as it made its way down.

"Probably a bit too hot just now, but give it a minute and it'll be just right unless you'd rather have a drink of… well, water is all I really have." Tam watched as tears streamed down Swamsoot's face and wondered at the balance between innocence and stupidity. "Water is good for you after all and there's nothing wrong with it on Scroat. In fact, there's a train of thought that says we should be bottling the spring water that keeps us healthy, as the posh ones apparently think it's the thing to drink now. Water. Can you imagine?"

"Posh ones?" Swamsoot enquired as he wiped the tears off his cheeks. "Posh ones is an unusual number, Tam."

"You're right there, sonny boy and don't let anyone tell you anything different. Those posh sorts from London are real unusual numbers, I'll tell you and the posh ones from Edinburgh… Weird is what I call them, but I must confess to being a bit parochial about the island." Swamsoot's portable whiz rod quickly picked out the explanation for being 'parochial about the island' and dropped it swiftly into a conversation.

"So precisely why are you so small-minded about the island, Tam?"

Tam winced. "Small-minded? I don't think I'm small-minded about the place, sonny. I just think I have a healthy protective element due to my preferred living conditions and surroundings. That plus the fact that the city folk are the real small-minded ones with their big cars and little phones and anything that shines."

"I see," replied the confused, young-looking traveller.

"John Murphy's son left here a nice enough young man, but he came back a pain in the backside with enough tales to turn anyone's head." Swamsoot pictured a young man with more than one tail, not like Jack but wondered exactly how many tails he could have. The draught caused by Jack's exuberant wagging was notable, but the notion of creating a draught to turn people's heads was mind-boggling to an alien not quite up to speed with the local lingo.

"How many tails did he have then, Tam?"

"Too many to count, I'd say and all of them stolen from high fliers, no doubt."

"Fascinating. You should tell me more about this trait, as it's not something we've personally encountered on Bellsurp. First of all, though, we need to negotiate a deal for me to sell you my goods, as you have no idea how to model yourself on anything other than dummies with less brain power than a dud battery." Tam watched him carefully as he made another attempt at the hot tea and repeated the burning trick.

"You're not that bright yourself, actually, are you, sonny boy? Keep going and you can take a layer of skin off the inside of your mouth."

It appeared that something of a hiatus had been reached in that Swamsoot needed time to control his emotions following the second scalding and Tam was somewhere in between liking and disliking the youngster sitting opposite him. "Do you want to go for a walk into the village and I'll buy some more biscuits for when your friends turn up?" Outside, his friends were working quietly and diligently without the need for Tam to know of their presence.

"That sounds like a good idea," Swamsoot answered. "Especially as I can get to meet some of the other idiots and explain their requirements to them, Tam."

Tam squinted. "Yes, I know just the people you can meet," he said and went for his coat and shoes. "In fact, as far as idiots are concerned, I can introduce you to some prime examples, sonny boy and most of them will have you eating out of their hands before you can sing the ballad of John and Yoko."

Swamsoot grimaced. "Really?" he asked for no reason.

"My God, yes. Some of them are pains in the…" Before he could complete the sentence, the door opened, whereupon Delius appeared wearing a smile of self-satisfaction.

"Complete, sir."

"Excellent," replied the proud captain. "I trust everything is to current standards and will meet local requirements?"

"Yes, sir. The whiz rod allowed us access to all local classifications and protocols and although some of them are very elemental in their detail and implementation, we have complied, sir."

"Splendid. You are dismissed, Delius and commend the men."

Delius smiled with a hint of arrogance. "They already know, sir. Thank you." And with that, he backed out of the door and joined the team to clear up and move everything back to the ship just as Tam re-entered.

"Were you speaking to me there, sonny boy?"

"No," Swamsoot answered without emotion and stood up as Tam began fastening his shoelaces.

"You know, I used to live with a woman who wouldn't let me put my shoes on in the house. Can you believe that?"

"Yes."

"Well, obviously, you can believe it, but it's all a bit unnecessary, isn't it?"

"Yes."

"I mean, if we were meant to walk around in our stocking feet all of the time, God would have given us tougher soles, wouldn't he?"

"Yes."

"Precisely." Tam finished fastening his laces as Swamsoot pondered the toughness of the soul and why God would have wanted it tougher simply because of a house-proud woman. "In fact, I couldn't sit on the settee when it was polished and not because it was too slippy."

"Really?" asked Swamsoot, now slightly more confused by the link of slippy furniture to shoe laces and Tam seemed determined to continue.

"Actually, once, when I came in from the pub, she made me undress at the door because I had been walking through the corn fields in the summer and I was covered in corn flies. Between you and me, sonny boy, I think she was a bit barmy, but then again, she lived with me, so she must have been slightly unbalanced." He grinned at the bemused young man standing in front of him, whom, not knowing any better, smiled back. "Right then, let's go and get some bits and pieces and I'll tell you more about her on the way, shall I?"

"Certainly, but will I eventually get an answer out of you with regard to the necessary purchase that will ultimately change your life from that equivalent to a hamster's intelligence to an average..."

"As it happens," interrupted Tam. "We go right past her parent's place and she sometimes comes to the island at this time of the year for a visit or two, mainly because it's a lovely time to see the place, don't you agree?"

"Absolutely, but we need to agree on a price for this..."

"And although I wouldn't like to share a house with her these days, it's always nice to see her." Tam stood up and towered over Swamsoot, who momentarily felt intimidated until the Scotsman spoke again, "Fancy another biscuit before we go?"

"No."

"No, what?" Tam asked like a schoolteacher.

"No biscuit," Swamsoot answered like a school pupil.

"No, thank you," Tam reminded him. It was clearly another human quirk he was unfamiliar with, so he guessed again.

"You're welcome."

Tam stared at him and muttered quietly about upbringings and opened the door at the front of the room to display the sea cutting into the land as softly as a baby sucking a thumb.

"Some view, eh?"

Ripples were sliding in and out, creating virtually no patterns on the shoreline and the sea took on a green hue with the reflection of the mountains on either side of the inlet. The horizon looked close enough to swim to and a light breeze flushed Swamsoot's face as he gazed wide-mouthed at the breathtaking view. Tam recognised the look as so often before visitors to the island were agog at the natural beauty on the coastline around Scroat. "I bet you don't have anything like that view where you're from, do you?" As he held the door open for his young visitor to follow him out of the house and on the path to the village, the remaining visitors cleared away everything as directed while Tam headed for the village, completely unaware that his last statement was the most literal he had ever made.

As girlfriends went, Ethel wasn't the best girlfriend he could have hoped for, although she wasn't actually his girlfriend and, in the truest sense, not really a girl. Swamsoot has tried his best to woo her the only way he knew, but wooing wasn't really a Bellsurpian strong point and before any progress was made, he suffered setbacks aplenty. Engaging the services of Calistones as go-betweens were always going to be a risk, but he decided the benefits would outweigh the risk as he sent Madder to eavesdrop on her thoughts before he called to see her.

"I believe she needs the toilet, sir," Madder told him earnestly as he approached him in the corridor that housed Ethel and other clever people of her ilk.

"I don't think I asked you about her toilet habits, did I?"

"Of course not, sir, but you didn't tell me not to find out about her toilet habits either." Seemed logical, in a Bellsurpian way, but Swamsoot has picked up traits that made him almost human in many ways, including common sense.

"Naturally," he started as Ethel opened her door behind him and out of his vision. "But why would I ask anyone to check anyone's toilet habits, particularly Ethel's?" Just as naturally, he was disappointed to hear the door slam shut behind him. "I should probably call back again, Madder."

"Never again, actually, sir. In fact, if ever you were considering suicide as an option…"

"Thank you, Madder. I can figure out how she's feeling right now without your wonderful mind tricks."

And with that, he left her apartment complex and went home to try another day. The next day, in fact and once more with Madder for company. "Just make sure she isn't coming to the door before we start discussing… well, anything really."

"Yes sir, sir," answered the obedient Calistone and began reading whatever thoughts were hidden behind the door. "Bad news, sir. I'm afraid she's dead."

"What?" Swamsoot shouted so loudly that the eavesdropper's committee sited in the building all submitted sick notes for red-ear. "Dead?"

"I'm afraid so, sir."

"Ethel," Swamsoot whispered with soft emotion as he kicked the door open to find the room empty. "Ethel," he repeated with a quota of curiosity now deep in his voice box as he ran around the rooms to find her elsewhere.

"Perhaps she's not dead after all, sir and she's just popped out to get the shopping or something." As sure as he could have guessed, Ethel returned to find Swamsoot and Madder in her apartment with the door swinging precariously on one twisted hinge. "That's correct, sir," Madder confirmed his thoughts discreetly. "Now is not a good time to ask for a date."

In anyone's thoughts, it was not a time to do anything except leave with the promise of a worker to put right the damage. For a frustrated young man, this was proving excruciating, but he was nothing if not persistent and the only way to a woman's heart, he deemed, was through perseverance and the pursuance of intolerable nuisance value. The very next day, he knocked on Ethel's door, softly.

"Hello, Ethel. I know this may seem inappropriate at this stage but…"

"Swamsoot!" she squawked with excitement. "Come in, please and read this dissertation."

It was a surprise to him. "Gosh," he said meekly. "This is a surprise."

"Not to me, it isn't, but I took the liberty of inviting Madder around and he mentioned that you were on the way here." Something stirred in him that, he deduced, might have been admiration, although it may have been more infatuation than cold, clinical admiration. "I have a chance to alter the way plans may be put into operation here and it might be a good idea to have one of the numbskull soldiers read it. Come in, please."

"Good idea, Ethel. One of the numbskull soldiers might just give a different perspective on… Oh, you mean me, don't you?"

"Absolutely, but don't feel offended by that as…"

"Excuse me, sir," Madder interrupted abruptly as he appeared from Ethel's kitchen. "I believe a serious pronouncement is about to be… pronounced."

Without as much as a 'tatty bye', Ethel donned her coat and headed for the door. As she escaped along the corridor, they faintly heard her say, 'If this is an early decision, I'll be furious. By the way, Madder…' Only her thoughts were passed on after that and Swamsoot looked at the pondering Calistone whilst he studied the flowing thoughts carefully.

"Well?" he asked impatiently.

After ten minutes, Madder gave his response. "Read the dissertation, sir," he answered as though thought information of that nature always took that level of time to pass on. Swamsoot knew better.

"Read the dissertation? Ten minutes to say, read the dissertation? I don't think so." Not given to moments of fervour, Swamsoot's face reddened as quickly as a greenhouse tomato in summer. "What else did she say then?"

Madder shuffled nervously. "It's a bit awkward, sir. Perhaps if you allowed me some time to make something to soften the blow, I could tell you what you want to hear?"

Swamsoot's brows lifted then dropped like a man smiling at his baby's first steps, followed by his baby's first major bowel movement on the carpet. "If you have something to tell me, Madder, I suggest you tell me what it is now and don't waste time dreaming up your version of events."

"My version of events, sir? I'm not sure I know what you mean." Only a mind reader with a minor skill threshold could have looked as guilty and Swamsoot wasn't having any of it.

"Madder, I think the time has come for you to obey an order now, so if you'd be so kind as to access my thought patterns to see how angry I'm becoming."

"Oh," stuttered the minion mind reader. "I didn't think... I thought... Perhaps if I simply explained what her thoughts are, sir." He didn't need further prompting. "Well, sir, it appears the lady of the house believes that only an idiot would carry out the task as designated in the outline plan and you fit the bill as you appear to be some kind of idiot in the view of the lady of the house. I should add, sir, that she does find your ridiculous inability to manage the most basic of social skills quite endearing. In fact, she believes that although skills like breathing and eating seem past your limited 'expertise' she does look upon you as a lovable idiot. "Actually..."

"I think I've heard everything I need to hear, Madder."

"Not quite, sir. Miss Balldytireskid also sees you as potential fodder for the laboratory when you arrive back from the mission if you are lucky enough to pass the skills test and be given the job in the first place."

"That's enough now, Madder."

"Apparently, sir, she also believes that, although she has met more than her fair share of imbeciles over the period of time since she sought employment with the clever people, she suspects you have the champion's hat, so to speak and won't let anyone down on the dim-witted front."

"Shut up now, Madder."

"If sir would like, I think I can manage to sketch how she sees the state of your ship after the mission as you're obviously, in her opinion, bound to land the vessel in a fire, sir. Actually…"

"Do you know how to obey orders, Madder, or are you just setting yourself up to be banished from the light to the dark?" Thoughts of the dark put Madder on his back foot; he was a Calistone, but even Calistones are Bellsurpians and, by default, scared of the dark.

"I understand, sir. Will there be anything else, sir?"

"You could try getting out?"

"Consider that order obeyed, sir." Madder promptly left Swamsoot sitting alone with the dissertation in his hand, wondering how she could think of him as an idiot. On the positive side, he mused, she also noted his lovable qualities, but the negatives in this particular depiction seemed to outweigh the positives, the way an ant measures up to a rhinoceros in the boxing ring and Swamsoot felt partly aggrieved.

Some way across town, though, Ethel was already sitting down to hear the news that would make or break her day. Within minutes, she was a broken woman and the plan to destroy Earth was becoming a reality and there was nothing she or the other clever people could do about it. Swamsoot had been volunteered for a job she felt certain he could never carry out to their satisfaction and the fallback would mean the obliteration of the target planet and the best she could do was ask questions.

"Excuse me," she hollered in her best hollering voice from the back of the packed auditorium. "Why are you intent on destroying this planet?"

An anonymous soldier fielded the query. It was traditional Bellsurpian behaviour to fashion a plot and then change the personnel each time it was debated. This process meant nobody was ever shouted at twice. Therefore, feelings were never hurt.

"We've intercepted a number of pieces of information about this planet and quite frankly, they don't appear to have any discernible qualities to interest clever people."

"That wasn't an answer," Ethel noted with a little acerbity, immediately terrifying half of the attendees and reducing the crowd by fifty per cent. "It was no more than a few patronising words. In fact, it wasn't even a few patronising words; it was a few pointless words said with a patronising tone."

"It's a good point you make there, but you seem to be overlooking the advantages of considering all options with the same level of commitment and drive and hopefully, we will all take what we want from it." As was also a stock-standard tradition on Bellsurp, a speech of such magnitude was greeted with great applause.

"Hang on," interrupted Ethel, now sporting a much redder face than the one she entered the room with. "You said absolutely nothing there. I propose to this conference that all justifiable, reportable, significant points identified by the mission captain be passed back to this conference before any decision be taken and that a quorum of ninety per cent of one hundred and twenty per cent of the overall agreed quorum be present and ratified before any action is taken. Clever people around the room dropped their heads almost apologetically as Ethel tied the soldiers in knots. "That way, if any destroying of civilisations takes place, you can all be given an opportunity to consider apposite theories in the way only big, strong, manly individuals such as yourself can make sense of."

As a soldier, he was classed as an idiot anyway. "Well…"

"I should point out, though, any glory or medals that go with a successful mission should be shared equally between all of the soldiers present, that way, not just one of you will receive the acclamation of the King." All of the clever people raised their impressed heads and watched the daft soldiers smiling at each other as Ethel went for the kill.

"Unless you'd prefer to take it back to your superiors to ratify and take to the King themselves?"

"We don't need anyone else to make our decisions for us." a voice from the back of the room shouted. "We're capable of making those things ourselves, those erm…"

"Decisions?" Ethel suggested helpfully, sensibly biting her wrist to stifle a giggle.

"Yes, decisions. We don't need someone else to make our decisions and take our medals and glory, do we, men?" A wave of recalcitrance rolled around the conference room as the clever people nodded deferentially at Ethel, who had managed to achieve something which might just save a civilisation many gortanties away. Dotted around the conference room were a number of Calistones who had been given the simple task of overseeing the security of a meeting where soldiers were meeting clever people; never a difficult task. In a situation such as this, however, each of the mind-reading sentinels were alerted to half of the room thinking of water flushing down a toilet pan. A skill such as theirs was suppressed with a little forethought and clever people had numerous tricks to keep their secrets safe. Within a minute, business was concluded and Ethel had forced through a plan that would be rescinded, albeit by order of the King only, as soon as General Battleprop realised his cunning plan had been hijacked. If she could get the flight off the ground, though, messages of congratulations could be sent to the King, meaning a u-turn would be somewhere between unlikely and impossible.

Best described as a mob, a team of clever people marched with Ethel as she returned to her home to find Swamsoot and prepare for the flight, which would take off in an hour.

"An hour? Have you lost your mind?" he asked as the beaming crowd of clever people watched her operating. "How could I possibly be prepared for a mission in one hour?"

Ethel batted her eyes, proving that a number of things passed the test of universal travel. "I just assumed you were... bright enough to be able to manage a mission that I have a real, personal interest in. I would be ever so grateful."

"I'm not silly enough to fall for that," he told her as he beckoned Melchione Madder to him. "I may be a little naive in some situations but..." His attention was momentarily averted to his most trusted Calistone. "Get me the list of all Calistones who..."

"Don't suffer from travel sickness, sir?"

"Yes. And stop…"

"Reading your mind, sir? Certainly, sir."

"Anyway," he carried on towards Ethel. "There are a number of reasons that I might want to embark on a mission such as this, but your charms aren't necessarily one of the reasons."

"That's a shame because I thought we might find a little time together before you leave."

Swamsoot stuttered and spat. "Not necessarily, I said. That doesn't mean they're not one of the reasons, specifically, just that it might look bad if I were to undertake a task…"

"I suspect you don't know what you're talking about now, so let's get to work and see what we can organise between us." The eager space captain instantly put a spring in his step and caught Madder in the corridor.

"Madder, I also need a list of all of those military…"

"Officers and enlisted sorts who can travel at short notice, sir."

"Yes and…"

"Stop reading your mind, sir?"

"Yes and bring me some lip mud, just in case I have to enter a kissathon before I leave."

Madder stared curiously. "I wasn't expecting that, sir."

Within thirty minutes, they had a crew assembled and Swamsoot looked at them with dismay; silence, he deemed, being the most appropriate way to voice his disapproval. More than one of his counterparts would consider the chance to move into deep space with this mob as lunacy or a flight of fancy only considered by special needs forces. Knowing a number of the assembled were Calistones, he tried with all of his might to concentrate on the belly button fluff he had managed to extract before jumping into a hot bath. Naturally, the Calistones read this as a past-time and spread the word that the captain was a keen knitter, choosing to weave his own home-spun wool. Odd, but a reason to giggle behind the boss's back when the time was right. Mobs such as this were normally cleared away from street corners and his only thought was how he would get them on to the craft without a number of accidental fatalities and he couldn't afford another scandal like that against his record.

"Right then… men and… It's not important how we address each other, just so long as we treat each other with respect and civility." He had already run out of things to say but knew that any positive sounds had to be disgorged without sending out sub-conscious messages of anxiety. "So what we need to do is create a situation of harmony whereby all members of this crew, whether they be men or whatsisname, can wander unhindered through the halls of power that we call Bob or Jim."

Absolute gibberish, he thought at the back of his mind whilst the front part accommodated the belly button fluff. First, Officer Delius touched him on the shoulder.

"I think that was absolute gibberish, sir."

"Mm," Swamsoot answered and raised his hands to accept the acclamation that went with any speech on Bellsurp, no matter how puerile. As expected, a standing ovation followed and he began ordering his officers to load the Space Ship Mollytots as Ethel and a troop of clever people entered the airstrip area. A common theme throughout the known universe, he felt his heart rate skip slightly quicker at the sight of the lovely Ethel, regardless of the unattractive company she kept.

"Hello," he said plainly, as she approached him, smiling like a… girl.

"Hello, captain. You look very organised here." Timing not being her best point, right on cue, two Calistones fell over each other and spilt a basket of fruit, sending a message of mild panic to their co-mind-readers, who panicked mildly in turn until the fruit had been recollected.

"Yes, things are going quite well as it happens, but let's just see if we can achieve whatever it is we set out to do." It sounded less than positive, but Ethel and her colleagues understood his apprehension due to the lack of information.

"I understand you will have to change the ship's name, but can we have a moment in private?" asked Ethel, raising hopes of a snog to the highest level yet, although the movement of her co-clever people towards his private quarters soon dashed any hopes he had of a truly private jamboree. "The thing is," she continued as the last of the party entered the small room and closed the door. "The plans are to stay nice and simple, although a number of your people will object to them."

"My people?" he asked, wondering if a pronouncement had been made affording him the title of King.

"The military sorts. They aren't going to be happy with the plan when they realise the King has approved no killing or annihilation of a planet of idiots, which is what they appear to be and obviously, nobody wants to protect idiots."

True to her timing expertise, Delius knocked on the door. "Do we have a toilet on board, sir?"

Swamsoot remained professional. "Follow the signs that say toilet."

Delius went away happy and Ethel continued. "It's this straightforward," she mentioned as casually as a horse lounging in a hay field. "You are to follow up on these messages, which we have intercepted in recent times and prove to the King that we can control these people in a very simple fashion and if we can't..."

"They will be killed," interjected a clever person he didn't recognise. "And we don't know how much time you have because Battleprop will undoubtedly want another mission to supersede your mission to ensure the killing comes first."

Swamsoot stared into Ethel's eyes and smiled. "Is that a new coat?" By his own naturally distracted standards, it wasn't that unusual a statement, but clever people only understood order and logic. "Only, I've never seen it before and it looks very nice, or at least it makes you look very nice."

A silent and shared look of puzzled faces stared at one another as Swamsoot carried on, flirting at an alarming rate. "In fact, if I had to say, I'd probably say I've never seen anyone look so stunning in a... How would you describe it, Ethel?"

"A white lab coat."

"Yes, that's a lovely way to describe it, a white lab coat. You certainly know how to carry it off."

"I see," Ethel answered untruthfully. "Perhaps we can get back to the mission now, as there's very little time to fill you in on the finite details."

"Certainly. Finite details?" Only his befuddled look gave the game away to the intelligent visitors.

"We have to explain what it is you'll be looking for and how you are to deal with the idiots when you find them. It's really very straightforward."

"Straightforward is good. I can do straightforward."

"Splendid," Ethel said without a hint of sarcasm. "I'm sure this will go very well and without any need for mass annihilation." Her jolly voice cheered up everyone in the room, including Swamsoot, as she possessed a remarkable skill for lighting up a room with a smile and, as far as Swamsoot was concerned, with the prospect of a kiss. Ethel, however, being a clever person, had never considered kissing anyone, not while there was thinking to do. They seemed a species apart, but being a soldier had taught him nothing, if not how to pester someone into submission.

Ethel produced a small pen-shaped object from her pocket and pointed it at the wall. "Look at this," she ordered him sweetly as a picture projected itself onto the wall behind him. "This gives us an idea of how stupid these people are."

A well-groomed man appeared in the picture with simple words for all to hear.

"Hurry or you'll miss the last day of our sale where we are giving furniture away. Look at these prices. Sofas only one-hundred and ninety-nine pounds and that's not all. This pine table and chairs a real give away at two-hundred and forty-nine pounds, but you better be quick. This is the last day of our seven-day bonanza where everything must go. Hurry along to Barbers furniture and tell them Tony sent you."

The scene ended with a sickly grin and a thumbs-up sign for all would-be punters.

"Interesting," Swamsoot noted with no interest.

"It's the epitome of how ridiculous these creatures are. This 'sale' he refers to has been going for four hundred of their days and this film is shown every day and still they turn up in huge numbers and purchase the goods he says he is giving away. He's an idiot, but the people to whom he is speaking are clearly bigger idiots because they believe him."

"Really?" asked Swamsoot with only the thoughts of a kiss crossing his mind.

"That's how we can succeed with simplicity itself. All you need to do is show that these people are being controlled with a mind control drug or telepathy and nobody can see them as a threat. If they can make mind-control drugs, we can make better mind-control drugs and all you have to do is get them to take our mind-control drugs and they will be ours to control. If you can use telepathy, even better. See? And it will give us an opportunity to dismantle the weapons they have produced that could blow up their whole planet and others besides."

"Well…"

"It isn't difficult, except for the speed of the mission, which is clearly going to be vital at every step, so you will need the perfect venue and probably a person with a position in their tribe that will enable you to attain the necessary support to get the thing moving."

It seemed understandable, even to a soldier. "So how do I get them to take the mind control drugs? And did you say weapons that can blow up planets?" It seemed a reasonable question from a high-ranking officer in an army who had never gotten close enough to an enemy to raise a fist in anger.

"See how easy that idiot gets then to buy his goods?" Ethel reminded him, casually ignoring the second part of the question. "How difficult can it be to make a better sales pitch than that idiot who has managed to convince them of a 'giveaway' that they have to pay for? It appears the more condescending you are, the easier the sell."

The clever person he didn't recognise interceded abruptly. "We have many examples for you to check on the way there so you will be well versed in the type of required approach by the time you arrive. It's almost impossible to fail in a mission so undemanding in thought processes, although we've even allowed for some erroneousness due to your military background being the type of factor we would be judged foolhardy to overlook. If you see what I mean?"

"It all seems very simple to me and I can hardly wait to get started, although it might be nice if I had a few minutes alone with Ethel to polish a few final points, so to speak."

A general nod of approval spun quickly around the small room and his pulse skipped a beat at the prospect of the much sought-after kiss happening eventually. As the rest of the clever people stood up to leave, Swamsoot swiftly repositioned himself on the seat next to her as the temperature climbed slightly upon hearing the door close behind them.

"Perhaps we could seal the deal with a little…"

"Right then," she interrupted tersely and opened up a small mechanical diary full of pop-up reminders. "This has all of the necessary information as well as a list of languages within a language decipherer that you can learn subconsciously any time of the day or night. It also includes a variety of mediums to which the idiots have become accustomed and utilise as a past-time of all things. You should learn them if for nothing other than 'fitting in' to ensure you gain their confidence at the sales pitch. In addition…"

Swamsoot took the bull by the horns. "I was hoping for a kiss."

Sweeping her hair across her face, she looked pensively at him, then at the pop-up diary. "I would have loaded something on if I had known you were that way inclined."

"A kiss from you, Ethel."

In an instant, the so-far professional meeting became an embarrassed silence as they looked at each other and then at their respective feet to avoid eye contact.

"Me?" she asked after an eternity. "Why would you want a kiss from me, Captain Swamsoot?"

"Because I find you enchanting and rather delightful to look at and I presume you kiss as well as you look."

It seemed like a full answer. "Oh," she muttered softly. "I had no idea that you felt that way about... Well, anyone, really."

"That's because you've never taken the time out to get to know me, or in fact, the time to look up from your books on clever stuff to see me staring at you from all different vantage points." Even Swamsoot felt a bit unnerved by the suggestion he had been stalking her. "When I say vantage points, I simply mean occasionally happening across you from time to time. You're not an infatuation, you understand."

"I see. Perhaps it would be inappropriate to continue the mission with this new-found knowledge in case the situation is compromised?"

"Oh no, that's not likely, unless you come along, of course, which you're welcome to do if you want, although you would have to pass a swift test on the relative..."

"I'm not about to undertake a lesson in intergalactic flight, Captain," she told him with the merest hint of a rebuke in her voice.

"Please, call me Damalgo," he encouraged her with a boyish glint in his eye.

"Why?"

"It's my name, actually. Damalgo Winstonian Swamsoot, from the Winstonian Institute Swamsoots."

"I think I'd prefer to call you captain if that's OK with you?" Ethel asked almost apologetically. "At least until you come back to a hero's welcome from Earth, then who knows?"

It was to be the one driving force he needed for the duration of the trip; that she left a sentence almost incomplete was as good as a hand in marriage in his mind and what he didn't know about the female mind wasn't worth knowing. She filled him in on the fine details of the mission and he made his final instructions to his team of officers and whatever else would travel with him. Minutes later, with the words ringing in his ears, he took off on a mission to save a planet from annihilation. Or to blow it up.

Watch Ya Step

Tam pointed at every beauty spot between his home and the village and with each opportunity, Swamsoot asked him to buy something worthless. If it hadn't been such a beautiful day, he might have become agitated by the whole affair, but in the main, Tam was a patient, understanding man. It went without saying, though, that he couldn't understand why Swamsoot was trying to sell him anything from toilet rolls to foreign holidays and all with the aplomb of a tired, uninspired salesman.

"See that rock with the boards crowded on top of it?" he asked the youngster, who was busy trawling his mind for his next sales pitch.

"Boards?"

"Local accent. Birds. We call them boards in these parts. Anyway, in the olden days, we would swim out there, plant a flag on Darcy's ledge, then swim back and the first one back won the village trophy for a year. One year, I won the trophy and climbed the furthest up the lardy pole. You couldn't catch me with a salmon hunter's net that year."

"I see," lied the highly confused Swamsoot. "Why would you think *I* could catch you with a net of any description?"

"I didn't mean you specifically. I simply meant I was a bit warm that year, although I was as thin as a racing snake and twice as fast as the man who threw stones at his own backside through the bathroom window." After a brief pause, Swamsoot decided not to even pretend he understood and instead tried another selling technique.

"Ever been to another country only to be struck down with terrible wind pains? Well, I have something here that will strengthen your resolve and enable you to go skiing and spend hours on a trampoline and don't be fooled by the price, which is a little less than nothing. In fact, I'll give you anything you want to take it off my hands."

"For God's sake, if it will shut you up, I'll play. What do you want me to do, though I'd rather play the sort of games I played when I was a kid?"

Swamsoot smiled broadly. "Do you mean you want to purchase whatever it is I have to sell?"

"Yes, let's get it over with. I'm actually growing a little bored." Another confusing image crossed his mind and he visualised a small bird growing in Tam's home.

"Right then," Swamsoot said keenly. "Let's get on with business."

"OK."

"I have a bowl of water here, which is essentially a bowl of water with nothing other than water in and looks and smells like water and…"

"Yes, it's a bowl of water."

"I'm prepared to sell it to you for a thousand pounds, although you can have it for nothing if you buy two." *An odd juxtaposition*, Tam thought but went along with the rather tiresome game. "OK, I'll have two for nothing."

"But to qualify for two, you have to give me three thousand pounds as a deposit."

"Will a cheque do?"

Swamsoot lowered his eyebrows in a frown. "Will a cheque do what?"

"Can I pay you with a cheque?"

The frown furrowed his brow. "I don't know," he answered and turned to leave. "I should go and find out, but I will require payment before you get your free water. Tam was mildly confused to watch Swamsoot disappear from view and over the hill towards home. Being of sound mind and body, the quiet Scot shrugged and made tracks towards the pub.

If nothing else, the pub always offered him a place to argue with grown-ups, rather than with youngsters like

Swamsoot. All things considered, however, Tam did find himself strangely fond of the young, inquisitive boy who had wandered off along a dangerous cliff-top all alone but seemingly capable of looking after himself. Or at least Tam felt a certain predilection towards confidence when considering the young man's ability to look after himself, though he didn't know why.

Of all the things he had never achieved, the skill of sixth sense had never come close, but still, he knew within himself that Swamsoot would make it safely to wherever he had come from. Inevitably, the question had to spring to mind as to just exactly where he had come from, but as ponderings went, this was a standard sort of ponder. That said, a youth, albeit with a group of other youths, should not have really appeared at his place without so much as an introduction.

Tam stood silently on the cliff-top path scratching his backside, then decided to carry on with the thoughts pushed to the back of his mind. "Mm," he muttered as he continued the leisurely pace to his local hostelry, where he was greeted by the usual groans of welcome as he pushed open the door.

"Good day, plebes." Nobody was particularly offended by his opening salvo as he had been using this particular salvo as long as anyone could remember and while it may have raised an eyebrow in the past, it didn't warrant a reaction of any sort now.

"Usual is it?" asked the ever-patient Milly Corwilly, even managing a smile with the customer service.

"Aye and I'll have a packet of crisps in case my young friend turns up. Cheese and pickle flavour, I think."

"Young friend, eh?" Milly asked, feigning interest. "Young woman, is it Tam or just a figment of your drunken imagination?"

"Just hand over the beer and crisps and not so much of your lip, young lassie or I'll be formally complaining to… whoever is in charge of this miserable place." As good as his attempt at social intercourse was, he succeeded only in bringing the temperature of the place down by a couple of degrees and further distanced himself from the people he disliked anyway. As hermit's lives went, Tam could have comfortably accentuated the lifestyle by simply following the same lifestyle modes he had adopted after a failed attempt at love some years prior.

He took his pint back to his designated seat in the window overlooking the beautiful inlet at Scroat bay and sat in silence, thinking about his young friend, conscious of the fact that he, as a responsible adult, should not have let a youngster wander off on a strange, dangerous path alone. For the first time in a long time, Tam found himself doing something which he recognised as an emotion or sensation he had experienced long ago. For the first time in a long time, he felt as though he should be doing something to make sure the young, annoying boy with a million pointless questions was safe and back to where he should be. For the first time in a long time, he sat in his local pub, not fancying his pint and not fancying an argument with the locals to whom he had grown accustomed without ever, over a period of time, growing to love them. For the first time in a long time, longer than he cared to remember, he worried.

Let's Do Lunch Or...

Ethel worried.

Ethel watched the monitors intently. Screens of all shapes and designs flashed a mixed batch of messages; some of them from a variety of missions around the galaxies that surrounded Bellsurp and mostly missions of the diplomatic sort and definitely none of them advising on how to begin a war with aliens. Aside from the inability to do anything other than shiver in the face of adversity, Bellsurpians had the knack of getting on with other races, an attribute that had carried them for meddlimants. Ethel was aware that this simple trait was a precious convention that should be protected and nurtured, but she and the other clever people had noticed the military folk coming up on the rails over a period of time and nobody appeared to have the will to challenge their intentions. That the clever people had hijacked the trip to Earth might well have been putting off the inevitable, but they had responsibilities to the nations of their planet and others. For days she had watched the screens and when all hope of a message from Swamsoot seemed lost, out of the blue, a question appeared.

HAVE BUYER. NEED TO KNOW WHAT I CAN OFFER HIM. DEAL DONE BUT HAVE REALISED I HAVE

Ethel squinted as she read the message and smiled sweetly at the thought of this man employed by the military but with as much aggression as two kittens fighting over the right to attack next door's bulldog. His message, though, was a real question and, more importantly, a question she didn't have an answer to. Without thought for her own safety, she swivelled in her chair and pressed a button, speaking quickly with excitement.

"Listen up, folks." She had watched a number of American dramas over the intergalactic whiz-rod and the spiel came easily. "Swamsoot has sent a message and we need as much brain power as we can muster as quickly as possible. We might have an emergency on our hands." As a clever person, she expected some questions pertaining to the message and at least one question on the intensity of the emergency. As a Bellsurpian, however, she should have looked out of the window first.

"But it's dark!"

"Can you come and get us, please?"

"I'm baking a cake and I'd hate to have it sink at this stage."

Darkness did create a surge of cowardice in Bellsurpians that only Bellsurpians understood and Ethel knew just how lily-livered these colleagues were, but for once in her life, she was demanding.

"As I have been ordained as a chief clever person on this project, I order you to meet up and come here in pairs right now. Anyone who doesn't make it here within thirty minutes will be formally removed from the clever person's panel and will have all clever privileges withdrawn forthwith. Do I make myself clear?" The silence across the radios and transmitters made it clear that she had indeed made herself clear.

Twelve hours later, when the Sun had risen in the North-West corner of the planet, the first of the clever people promptly arrived and set about making the tea. One by one, they turned up without sign of guilt or culpability for any danger their reluctance to venture out under cover of darkness may have caused Swamsoot. Of all of the things she had been frustrated by in the world of clever people, she knew getting the super-intelligent to walk out in the dark was more difficult than shovelling a rising tide back with a pitch-fork. Like all clever people before her, she bit her lip and decided to carry on without implementing the previous night's threats.

"Captain Swamsoot," she stated forcefully. "Has sent a very serious message which should be of real concern to us all but should be of particular concern to our provisions officer. Apparently, he has made contact with one of the idiots who seems keen to purchase some goods and he has no goods to offer for sale." As a man or Bellsurpian, the group turned to look at Welton Majesticka, the best-paid provisions officer South of the North(ish) point of Glinto. "Perhaps Welton would like to explain how the *provisions* for a mission based on selling goods as *provided* by the *provisions* officer weren't *provided*."

"Well, you can hardly blame me, can you?" Welton answered quickly in his defence. The strong silence that followed was broken only when Ethel realised nobody else was going to question it.

"What do you mean we can't blame you? Who do you recommend we blame, then?"

Welton thought briefly, then answered confidently. "Him," he said, pointing at the hardware inventor. A ripple of support went up for the claim because Seemon Chiselffrash, the hardware supplier, was as unpopular as anyone in the clever fraternity and boasted about his genius to the point of annoyance.

"What do you mean, him?" Ethel asked.

"Well, he told me it wasn't necessary to provide specific provisions due to the proclivity for things 'not normal' within the realms of the armed forces types." For a bunch of clever people, the majority seemed much too easily mollified by a one-liner as empty as that particular one-liner. Only Ethel seemed unimpressed.

"I think you should try harder than that," she noted, with the pitch in her voice rising ever higher. "We have more than ourselves to consider here unless you've failed to remember what the mission is about from our perspective?" Although the silence was a little off-putting, she carried on bravely. "We, albeit at short notice, put together a plan by utilising all of the best brains in Bellsurp and we can't muster the know-how to include the most important part of the plan. All we… allow me to correct myself. All you," she repeated, venomously pointing at the hardware supplier and the provisions officer. "had to do was ensure the saleable part of the function was on board with the military sorts who, as we all know, can not be relied upon to remember these things themselves. Is anyone else as frustrated as me at this point?"

Benjamin Daisy spoke for the first time. "I feel as though a breakdown in communication has been brought on by a variance of factors, most of which can be explained away as misinterpretation, but just as much requiring a much deeper though alignment catalogued for our research files and held in a secure environment whereby further and more extensive investigations can be employed to ascertain exactly where the breakdown came and whether or not a mathematical equation can be formally endorsed to ensure no such repeat can be assumed or expected in the future."

It felt wrong to Ethel but before she could drag it back, the room escalated into a forum for deliberation that only the keenest minds would understand and only the brain-dead would listen to.

"I suspect," came a voice from the back. "We may be following a premise that allows nothing for external influences here that might propagate a scenario that has hallmarks, dare I say, with influential fingerprints on it, if you know what I mean?" Naturally, nobody knew what he meant because it was gibberish. For a clever person to admit to not knowing what somebody meant, however, was professional suicide.

An anonymous voice shouted, "It's a good point."

"Well made," another spoke proudly.

Ethel inhaled deeply and just as deeply made the necessary attempt to bury her indignation and anger. As with all clever people get-togethers, nothing remotely resembling practicality came to the surface and she knew in her heart that the meeting goers would now take over procedures and she cursed herself for allowing it to happen. Amongst the various meetings over the years, she could only remember one ending with an outcome, but the likelihood of another meeting being called to discuss the burning building in which they were meeting was slim. Resigned to the abject refusal for action, she decided a shock tactic was the only option available to her.

"Unless we get some provisions to the ship on the Earth planet, the mission will fail and if it fails, the military will intercede and will summarily reduce the whole planet to rubble. That has more than a moral issue attached to it because my most recent investigations show that the rubble will be drawn into the fourth quadrant and we will subsequently be bombarded with meteors as large as Bellsurp itself. We could face annihilation unless we act immediately." As shock tactics went, it was pretty shocking and although she knew it would take only a small amount of research to counter her claim, she hoped it would be sufficient to have them roar into action and have provisions sent forthwith. Even top clevers such as Benjamin Daisy were shocked.

"If I may be so bold as to suggest," started the well-respected smart arse. "I think organising a meeting to consider the options in detail may be appropriate, particularly if our lives depend on it."

It made sense to everyone except Ethel.

"No, we can't organise a meeting to discuss something when it requires our urgent attention and the military sorts are virtually queuing up to take over where we slip up." A heartfelt thought indeed, but the clever people were renowned for their fortitude when it came to arranging meetings and all diaries were on knees around the room.

"I can do Friday at four."

"No good, I have a lesson for the under-nourished. What about Saturday at eleven?"

"Saturday? What are we, manual workers?"

"What about an evening meeting and we can arrange a bite to eat?"

A murmur of approval followed but was quickly washed away. "It gets dark pretty early at this time of year and we don't want to be walking home in the twilight, do we?"

"I can do any time that doesn't clash with the highlighting of Venus crossing the palava with Mars and Weepitahh."

Ethel had heard enough. "Right then, unless somebody, anybody, can suggest something practical to aid the mission, I'll simply have to do it all myself. How does that sound?" It actually sounded OK, but clever people didn't like to concede a point that easily.

"I think we should arrange a meeting to carefully consider what Ethel has suggested."

"Good idea, but as she is officially in charge of this operation, we shall have to have a quorum."

"Agreed. Is the quorum counter available any time soon so we can make the necessary arrangements to have him present? I'd hate to think we have to make another arrangement when we could have all business concluded on this particular matter unless…" Ethel heard no more on the subject as the door closed behind her.

Amongst the finest minds on Bellsurp was a finely tuned bureaucratic gene that could sniff out a paper exercise from the other side of the planet and turn a day-to-day task into an intergalactic incident. As a clever person, she protected herself and her own, yet as a Bellsurpian with a realistic take on life, she hated them all. Swamsoot was stranded on a strange planet many moons away with a motley crew of someone else's compiling and she felt as though she was the only one who could do something to help him and the people he had gone to kill.

Slumping back into the seat in front of the bank of computers, she noticed another message was waiting.

IT APPEARS THAT THESE IDIOTS HAVE A SELECTION OF ESTABLISHMENTS WHERE INFORMATION CAN BE SOUGHT. AS I AWAIT YOUR INSTRUCTIONS, I WILL INVESTIGATE. TELEVISION APPEARS TO BE POPULAR, SO I WILL BEGIN THERE AND PROGRESS TO LIBRARIES.

CAPTAIN DAMALGO WINSTONIAN SWAMSOOT

Seemed harmless to Ethel, who put on her thinking cap and tried to devise a way to send provisions that could arrive before the military missiles destroyed everything Swamsoot was trying to save. Just to confuse matters more, feeling isolated by her bright colleagues, Ethel wondered what the emotion she was experiencing was related to. Swamsoot had entered her life from a strange angle and had made a mess of every opportunity to engage her in the simplest of social associations, yet still, she felt a pang of sentimentality towards him every time she pictured him marching up the gangway to his vessel the day he left.

Never having before experienced such a sensation towards a fellow Bellsurpian, she stuck her finger in the Emotion Deducer and waited patiently for the results. Within a few short seconds, the small machine beeped, notifying her of the result. Emotion Deducers had been invented by one of the clever people after the group as a whole came under attack from the Bellsurpian masses for being too cold and mechanical in their outlook on life and all clever people sported the device on their office desks thus enabling a change in deportment should the need arise. As well as showing the clever people up as a much more caring bunch, it had proved priceless in the pursuit of an understanding of teenage Bellsurpians at tea time but was unable to help Bellsurpian husbands understand their wives. It was only a machine after all.

As with all robotic instruments, the Emotion Deducer was basic with the information it was prepared to provide and this was no exception. 'Affection', it said with a monotone blandness that only underlined the irony of a machine that was designed to improve social skills.

"Interesting," Ethel said to herself.

'No, you are not,' answered the machine before she had the chance to remove her finger. "Hmm," she whispered out of earshot and wondered why the machine that was never wrong would now prove to be so. As with many a Bellsurpian woman, when faced with a heavy day's thought, Ethel turned to confectionary and began nibbling at a bar of sweet, dark brown, milky substance and smiled contentedly.

The Best in the Business

Swamsoot watched the television as if his life depended upon it. That his life might well have depended on it was not really a thought he wanted to contemplate, but all things being equal, the television was great entertainment, albeit peppered with the ludicrous advertisements that had become something of a nemesis to him.

Accessing the channels had been very straightforward and enlightening; easy free access for a race so badly advanced. 'Strange bunch of… not individuals', he mused and wondered why they were so intent on doing the same as each other and with such unabated duplication. Back home on Bellsurp, copying your neighbour was frowned upon and in bad cases, the village frowner would be asked to fluff up his bushiest eyebrow hair and frown for hours at copycats. Without specific provisions, he faced an uphill struggle to convince the humans to purchase something he didn't have and although Tam had seemed keen to do so, he was never confident the deal was in the bag. Bellsurpians, though, were equivalent to being unnecessarily optimistic at the wrong times and just as his mind began to waiver, an advertisement gave him an idea.

CALL THIS NUMBER NOW BEFORE YOUR CHANCE FOR A MILLION GOES TO SOMEONE ELSE. SIMPLY ANSWER THIS QUESTION AND RING 0707070555070. CALLS COST £2 PER MINUTE

Brilliant, thought Swamsoot, only to be further enlightened by the quieter sequel.

CALL DURATION MINIMUM SIX MINUTES. MOBILE CALLS COST MAY VARY GREATLY. UNDER 16s MUST SEEK PERMISSION OF THE PERSON WHO PAYS THE TELEPHONE BILL

His viewing screen flashed automatically from channel to channel and his mind raced just as quickly to keep up with it, simultaneously pressing his call button to bring Delius rushing to his side.

"How may I help, sir?"

"Delius," he started casually. "I need you to set up a communication link in line with the human's mobile telecommunication networks, thus enabling us to offer a prize that doesn't exist via their television networks." Delius had taken the time to do not a little homework himself and brightened at the potential prospects.

"Might we get to meet Laurel and Hardy, sir?"

Swamsoot considered this as a morale booster. "Possibly. If we achieve all that we set out to do, I'll make the necessary arrangements to meet Laurel and Hardy."

"Splendid, sir. I'll go and tell the network crews immediately and get them working right now." As though dragged back by a piece of elastic, he posed Swamsoot an awkward question of the 'I wasn't expecting that' variety. "If I'm allowed to enquire, sir, precisely what is it that we're trying to achieve here on Earth?"

The pause was monstrous. "Well," he started eventually. "If we manage to sell something to the humans to demonstrate that they can be easily swayed and therefore not a risk to the security of themselves or neighbouring communities, we can go home."

"I see," Delius lied. "Sounds a bit… unlikely, sir, if I may be so bold as to suggest such a thing." Swamsoot scratched his head and rubbed his nose and thought about the explanation that felt ridiculous before he started giving it.

"Do you have any Calistone genes, Delius?"

"No, sir," answered his subordinate with a hint of pomposity. "All of my family background is pure Bellsurp with just a hint of dragon, sir."

"I see," Swamsoot replied untruthfully, comfortable with the knowledge that he could lie and get away with it. On balance, he decided not to lie, though and instead decided honesty was the best option. "You're right, though, Delius. In fact, that's probably just about the most sensible thing I've heard since we left Bellsurp, although, in fairness, it hasn't got much in the way of competition. Have you been on many missions, Delius?"

"No, sir. This is only my fifteenth mission, including the training missions to places like Jenka to catch the killer bugs of Horteen."

"I see. And how many of the fifteen were training missions to Jenka to catch the killer bugs of Horteen?"

"Fourteen, sir."

"Splendid. My most experienced officer is enjoying his first authentic trip into the unknown."

"Sorry, sir. If I had known you wanted more experienced officers, I would have lied when you asked the question."

Swamsoot blushed. "It's not your fault, Delius. I had a chance to put a little more time and effort in to picking some of the crew and I should have picked some more experience where I needed it." Not being Calistone himself, Swamsoot was a little unnerved to sense a feeling of guilt and decided a bit of integrity would go a long way with Delius. "The thing is, we appear to be on a very difficult mission here, Delius and I wasn't expecting it to be this difficult. That said, I think if you and I get our thinking caps on," both men turned their heads to see the thinking caps hanging on the wall, "I'm confident we can do everything we need here and can go home as heroes," Delius smiled. Of all the bosses he had worked for, Swamsoot was the only one who instilled genuine confidence in all of his crew. Delius smiled because he knew the mission was in safe hands.

At the same time, fifteen generals sat staring at blank screens back on Bellsurp, mourning the loss of good men and Calistones.

"I never enjoy this part of the job," General Battleprop opened with and drew a collective grumble of agreement from the uniforms around the long, dark, stained table. "If there was any way we could warn him, I would be happy to do so and at least give him a chance to get his crew off that infernal planet before we blow it into a million pieces."

Great Minds and All That...

Secrets formed a huge part of the Bellsurpian culture. Trying to keep one, however, was as easy as carrying a horse on a handful of steam and just *getting* a handful was difficult enough. Inevitably, the information was leaked to the clever people that planet Earth was going to be eradicated, thus saving all surrounding space-communities mountains of a hassle for the future and saving Bellsurpians from having to file a report when the mission arrived home.

"How can we allow it to happen?" asked Ethel.

"How can we stop it without a meeting of your people?" replied Bamber Wetbot. "I'm Damalgo's best friend and nobody wants to get him home safely more than me, but I think the clever people are the only ones who can think up something to stop this."

"But they have meetings about meetings and we don't have enough time for that, do we?"

Bamber scratched his head studiously. "What about emergency meetings?" he asked honestly and innocently as he climbed out of his seat to look out of the window across the hills of Baronfergus where he and Swamsoot played as children hundreds of years ago.

"The last emergency meeting they were called to was cancelled because a thunderstorm was forecast in the next space sector. It eventually convened four days later and decided that the word emergency was too generic and that any future emergency meetings would have to be formally ratified by the emergency committee."

"Well, what about going to the emergency committee directly then?"

"Unfortunately, they didn't get round to picking the committee because that would have meant calling it an emergency committee and that particular phrase was too generic."

Bamber thought for a moment. "You're not terribly clever for clever people, are you? No offence meant, of course."

"None taken," she answered casually with a wave of her hand. If she had learnt anything in recent times, it was that accepting other people's views would mean criticism for the simple reason that the clever people weren't really that clever. Naturally, they were clever in the traditional sense, but that only meant they could work things out that nobody understood. In itself, that was fine as it allowed them so much autonomy that even if others had understood their workings, they would never question it. However, now that she was faced with a practical problem, she realised just how inadequate and positively sterile the group was.

Deep down, and not really that deep, she knew it all along but allowing the workings of a few egg-heads to bamboozle the masses seemed as harmless as a gentle amble along the seafront of her hometown in Wellingtonish where the purple sea met the green sky forming points of light as sharp as laser beams. Such natural beauty was unique on Bellsurp, where the changing planet's atmosphere and harmful gases created mainly ugly skylines. Looking over Bamber's shoulder, she could make out a cloud on the distant horizon.

"There's a cloud looming anyway, so even trying to get them out would be a task in itself." Bamber noticed the distant shade in the sky and thought about making a sarcastic comment on the clever people's cowardice. Never having contemplated anything vaguely brave himself, though, he decided on prudence and agreed with the increasingly frantic Ethel.

"Well, Ethel, we appear to be alone here, so let's get down to work and devise a plan that will ensure my friend and your lover gets home safely."

Ethel leant forward and spun Bamber around to face her. "My lover?"

"Damalgo," he answered nonchalantly and carried on without bewilderment or surprise. "And if we can't get him home safely, we need to get him and his crew to a place where we…"

"What do you mean, my lover?"

"Damalgo," he answered again, reinforcing his position on the matter.

"But…" Another flaw in the clever makeup was a lack of clarity when flustered. "But I'm not… that is, he's not… We aren't even…" For no good reason, she noticed how very quiet it was here and that the temperature had climbed by a few degrees and was just touching unbearable. "Why would you think that Captain Swamsoot and I are lovers, Bamber?"

Bamber smiled, "Just look at you. You're like a two-hundred-year-old blushing and getting all flustered and breathless every time you think about him."

"I am not," she answered, getting all flustered and breathless as she thought about him. "Captain Swamsoot and I happen to share a principle in relation to this particular mission and we both believe the annihilation of a whole race is barbaric and avoidable." She moved carefully to a seat in the centre of the room and sat uneasily in it while Bamber turned slowly with a huge grin on his cheeky face.

Bamber Wetbot and Swamsoot were distinctly similar and had started school together, carried on through camps, military and civilian and mirrored each other's progress as they went. That they copied each other's results during exams played a big part in that, but even so, they were alike to the extent they were often confused for each other. His eyebrows touched as his grin widened. "Listen, Ethel, if you say you aren't in love with Damalgo that's fine by me, as long as you're convinced you can deal with this problem in a cold and impartial manner.

Not normally the emotional type, Ethel reacted. "Excuse me, Bamber Wetbot, but I am not the type to go all gooey because a being of the opposite gender happens to be charming and attractive in a rough and docile sort of way. In fact, Captain Swamsoot has made more basic errors trying to woo me than any other suitor I have ever had the misfortune to reject."

Bamber rubbed his chin thoughtfully. "I see," he lied. "And I suppose you think Damalgo is another suitor to reject? So, if I may be so bold as to inquire, how many suitors have actually come calling over the years?"

Ethel blushed, then moved on business-like. "We have a situation here that requires some real thinking and action, Bamber and the notion that I would waste this valuable time chatting idly about my various courtships is something of a nonsense. Let's get to work and cut this idle chit-chat out right now."

Bamber raised his hands in surrender. "Fine by me, but I was just interested because I know Damalgo is very fond of you and he does have a soft spot for opposite genders with an unbroken heart if you know what I mean?"

Ethel had no clue what he meant. "I know what you mean," she answered untruthfully.

"So?"

"So what?" she echoed the sentiment.

"So, have you had your heart broken in the past by some fly-by-night warrior with no feelings?"

"Bamber, that's none of your concern." Ethel's face was giving away much more than her officious tones and Bamber Wetbot went in tactfully for the answer he was interested in for the sake of his own curiosity only.

"Well, answer me just one question then, Ethel. If I was to ask you just exactly how many opposite genders you've fallen in love with, would you tell me if I didn't ask for names and addresses?" Ethel mused carefully as he put on the pressure. "I assume that your feelings for Damalgo are at least fondness and until you're comfortable to discuss anything further on the matter, I'll respect your privacy. Obviously, I have no interest in your feelings over and above fondness for anyone of the opposite gender and I will be more than willing to hear what you have to say and simply cast the information from my mind leaving it a secret virtually untouched."

"Aha!" Ethel squawked. Being a clever sort meant she would never be able to deal with gibberish of any sort, as her thought-patterns were based on systems more akin to binary classifications rather than the smart tongue of a casual shirker like Bamber Wetbot.

"So all you need to tell me is exactly how many of the opposite gender have you been wooed by in the, let's say, past one hundred and fifty years?"

"Including Captain Swamsoot?" she asked with a level of interest peeping over the emotional parapet.

"Yes, including Damalgo."

Being a clever person, her thought patterns were almost visible as she rolled her eyes around in her head like a legless hamster caught in a wheel. "Well, including Captain Swamsoot… one." Bamber raised his finger to make a tacit point when she pre-empted his assertion with a shaking finger of her own. "But clever people are restricted in the amount of social contact we are allowed to have due to the thought patterns that could be abused by the Calistones."

"Really?" asked Bamber, showing an interest in someone other than himself for a change.

"Absolutely. In fact, if the Calistones were to get a grip on our thought patterns, we could lose control of the planet." The words were barely out of her mouth when Ethel realised what she had said was a mistake. "So we really need to develop a process to bring them home safely and without drawing attention to you and me, I suppose."

Bamber baulked. "Lose control of the planet?" he asked plainly.

"What we need to consider is the effect any plan might have on..."

"Hold it, Ethel. Did you just say you might lose control of the planet if the Calistones were to read some clever people's minds?"

Ethel paused and stared deep into Bamber's eyes. "No," she stated almost categorically. "Not that any of that is important, of course. What we need to do is organise ourselves properly and make sure we devise an appropriate plan." And in that matter-of-fact answer, the moment was gone and Bamber had missed the opportunity to make inroads into the workings of his planet, which he barely understood at the best of times. What he missed out on was the chance to quiz her on what made the planet tick, what the meaning of the Bellsurpian existence was and how they get those small holes at the end of needles. With a step up in pace, Ethel sucked in a lungful of air and spat out a mouthful of cures without any detail.

"I have an idea. If we…then all we need to do is… of course, he'll have to convince them that… I think we can get away with it, Bamber. I really do, provided he can just… Yes, I think it will work." As was the way when the clever people met the military people, the armed forces personnel spent the bulk of the time pretending not to be stupid. As the irony of the term 'military intelligence' passed Bellsurpians by, the militia plodded through life, convinced that the world had faith in them to the furthest degree. In fairness, only clever people were aware of the shortcomings. As with all head-strong pompous buffoons, the clever people believed everyone had complete faith in *them*. Such was the finite balance in Bellsurpian society, clever people and military people trusted nobody, but themselves and these two were no exception. Tonight they would attempt to devise a plan for a mutual friend's sake and at the same time, they would find it increasingly difficult to agree to anything. As they began a two-person crusade for salvation, Swamsoot moved ever closer to annihilation.

Just a Minute

"I think I have the answer to this problem," Tam noted wryly. "If we can get the idiot opposite me to pay attention to the card game and stop staring out of the window."

"I can't help it," Billy McJack answered quickly. "I'm sure I saw a helicopter hovering around before and I don't know where it was going, which is a bit of a worry to a man in my position."

"What, you mean the local nosey neighbour?" Eddie Fischwick added without taking his eyes off his playing cards.

"It is a very responsible position, Billy," Geordie Ticker added to the debate with a devil's grin parting his lips. "If we didn't have someone in your job, we'd never know when Agnes buys her pastries."

"Or her washing powder," Tam threw in for good measure.

Billy moved swiftly to squash the rebellion. "All right, all right. Just because you have no respect for the law on this island doesn't mean you can ridicule the uniform, gentlemen." As if well-rehearsed, all three looked at each other and then over their respective shoulders for any visiting gentlemen. Billy raised his head again and shrugged his shoulders. His broad shoulders almost filled the window in which they sat playing a friendly card game that usually degenerated into a battle royale that Billy would win ten times out of ten. Hands the size of dinner plates held the cards like others held postage stamps and his dark sunken eyes surrounded by an overhanging fringe gave something of a menacing look to the island's constabulary, a title he held solely since his sergeant retired some four years prior.

"It just struck me as being a bit unusual, that's all, seeing a helicopter when it's not a Friday and I don't know of any special provisions order being made." His partners demonstrated no real interest, but Tam offered a speck of curiosity in order to keep the game going.

"Perhaps the school trip came by helicopter. God knows the kids these days travel in ways that we're not used to."

"School trip?" Billy asked. "Nobody told me about any school trip to the island today and if they've brought kids over here without telling me there's going to be trouble for someone, I can tell you."

"Well, play a card before you start trouble." Geordie reminded sternly. "And as soon as you've done it, go to the bar and get the drinks, will you?"

"I didn't know there was a school trip either, Tam," Eddie mentioned casually. "And I'm sure Marion would have mentioned it to me if there was one. Being the school teacher on this island doesn't create too much excitement for her and I can't imagine her keeping that to herself over the dinner table."

"Well, there's a trip, all right, because they've been to my place. One of them is a young kid with a smart mouth, but sort of... pleasant, if you know what I mean?"

"So, how many of them are there?" Billy asked as if registering concern over an un-notified trip to 'his' island.

"Don't know, really. There seemed to be a few of them in my garden before, but I didn't really..." Tam's voice trailed off as the card school lifted their heads, waiting for the end of the sentence. "I'm not really sure that I saw the rest of them, well I mean, I saw them, I must have seen them, but I can't really remember how many... or what they looked like or..."

"At least you've got the drink under control, Tam."

"What? Oh, yes, the drink." Their card games often ended without an outcome as a leisurely pastime drifted into oblivion, but it usually lasted longer than it had so far today.

Tam stood up. "I've just remembered that I need to see to the dog," he said as he made a move towards the door. "As well as washing the dishes and putting the…" His voice disappeared with him through the doorway and the card school sat back and perused the scene in their individual styles. Billy McJack rubbed his chin thoughtfully but kept his suspicions to himself. On the opposite side of the table, Eddie Fischwick presumed he had misheard Tam saying he was going to wash the dishes whilst Geordie Ticker cursed silently over the first decent hand of cards he had picked up for three weeks.

A Flash of Genius

Ethel looked at the book and tempered her apprehension with the options available to her, which numbered zero. After hours of contemplation, neither Bamber nor her had managed as much as a suggestion in relation to a life-saving initiative. Every thought that had passed through his head was tinged with additional thoughts of becoming a hero and having Bellsurpian girls wanting him for reasons he wouldn't dare discuss with his parents.

Ethel thought only of how she was letting everyone down, particularly herself, by her inability to think up a plan to mend this broken mission plan. Clever people only really had one job and that was to fix broken things or invent new things. This mission was a thing and it needed some clever thought to get it back on track and only a flash of inspiration was going to darn the hole in this mission's metaphorical sock.

Ethel looked at Bamber and he returned the stare with interest and as with all flashes of inspiration, the bulb came on and out gushed the idea.

"I've got it!" shouted Bamber surprisingly.

"Eh? *You've* got it?"

"Yes, I've got it. If we manage to get a…"

"I've got it!" Ethel interrupted as if spurred on by the brainwaves of an inferior military numbskull. "If we manage to send down something they can believe in, we can conjure up a position of supplication that will at least give the impression of hierarchy doing what hierarchy should do and if they can proliferate beyond the community, then they might just create the impression of what will at least look like they've conquered a less well-educated race and that they might endure changes to their outlooks on life at home and in the other universes."

Bamber stared in silence momentarily. "Well, I was…"

"Sorry, Bamber, is that what you were about to say?"

"Actually, I was going to say if we manage to get another biscuit on top of this pile, we'll have the platoon biscuit balancing record." Both Ethel and Bamber had the good grace to look slightly embarrassed and Ethel moved on to develop her plan further as Bamber built a small house of shortbread. If that didn't offer solace to Swamsoot, nothing would. Although Swamsoot it was who held the current biscuit record and if that went while he was away, he would be furious.

I Never Touched It

Tam walked home as slowly as he had walked to the pub with the confused thoughts of his visitors at the fore of his mind and wondered what he had imagined and what was real. Being an intelligent man, he knew the passage to the island would have been discussed with at least the island constabulary and being a school group, the island's best-known teacher would have some knowledge. Why, then had nobody been made aware? Why was Swamsoot so cheeky and… 'Stop asking yourself questions', he thought as he approached Mariner's bend, a point from which he would see his home and the place where he felt most at ease in the world.

A light fret washed across his face, followed by a warm breeze bringing in the smell of the sea that everyone commented on when visiting the island of Scroat. Many had even commented on feeling 'dreamy', such was the beauty of this part of the island and some had even commented on the cool breeze creating that sensation of wanting to curl up in front of a log fire and… 'Cool breeze', he said to himself. 'Warm breeze', he followed up with. Amongst the list of attractions listed in the tourist office on the island of Scroat, 'warm breezes rolling in from the sea creating a sensation of well-being' did not feature. If truth be told, the tourist attractions of Scroat numbered only the walks around the numerous paths overlooking the coastline. Of all of the available walks, each of them was accompanied by cold, blustery winds except during the summer, which usually came midweek in July or August. Tam scratched his head and looked across to his home. 'Odd', he mused and quickened his step towards his hillside cottage with the sea views and wondered when he had the extension built. Things were becoming very strange on the island of Scroat.

As Long As You Don't Say…

"If we convince the people on the planet Earth that a terrible fate was about to befall them and that Damalgo Winstonian Swamsoot was the man to save them, perhaps they would conform?"

"Hmm?"

"Bamber, will you pay attention, please? We are supposed to be devising a plan to save the crew on Swamsoot's mission as well as the indigenous creatures on the planet he's visiting."

Bamber nodded and lifted his head from his comic. "Yes, I realise that Ethel, but jumping, Jessie is about to fly over the cosmic stadium with the glow-torch to break out…" Thankfully he noticed the look of irritation on her face and recognised the disdain that accompanied it. "Well, perhaps the television can wait."

"Right then, Bamber. How does this sound to you? As you know, Swamsoot has to be able to get a high level of conformity from that lot down there to the extent that he can demonstrate we can induce mind control that would ultimately exhibit sufficient by way of authority to justify the continued existence with the removal of the fear factor that currently concerns your bosses in the military establishment. OK?”

“OK,” Bamber responded blandly as his eyes glazed over like a bored shark taking a bite out of its fifteenth haddock of the day. “If you’re sure.”

“What do you mean, if I’m sure? Of course, I’m sure. You attended the same meetings as me, didn’t you?”

Bamber nodded sheepishly. “Well, yes, but I don’t usually stay awake at these meetings and besides, Damalgo tells me what I’ve missed, so it’s pointless us both being bored.”

Ethel scowled but went on unabated. “In any event, I believe I have the plan to give his mission a fighting chance and I’ve sent a message saying that just a couple of minutes ago.”

“What?” Bamber asked with an unusual level of urgency in his voice.

“I’ve just sent a message on the whiz rod to tell them I think we have a fighting chance of a solution.”

“Is that how you worded it?”

“Well…”

"Did you use the word 'fighting' in the message?" he asked, his voice becoming slightly breathless at her expected response.

"Well, yes."

"Oh, dear!"

Do You Want the Good News Or...

Swamsoot had stepped off the craft and headed back towards Tam's place to see if he could put more pressure on the middle-aged Scot to buy something he didn't need. Perhaps if he hadn't seen the face of the Calistone security guards at the base of the ramp, he wouldn't have known anything.

"What's wrong?" he asked reasonably. "What are you picking up?" But it was too late. Both Calistone men had turned and headed for the hills and Swamsoot wasn't quick enough to get off the ramp before he was trampled by all crew members rolling over the top of him like a tide rolls over a washed-up sock at the seaside. Tumbling helplessly, he recognised a pair of trousers and hung on gamely to Sergeant Delius' pants until he could look him straight in the eye at ground level.

"Sergeant Delius. What the blue moons is going on?"

"Message, sir. Too dangerous. Must run. Must hide. Must…"

A sharp punch to the nose stopped the gibbering. "Take a deep breath and tell me what is happening. Understand?"

Delius duly obeyed. "We have received a message from Bellsurp, sir, stating that we are to have a fight with… Well, it doesn't actually state who the fight is with, but it's from one of the clever people, sir and they would know and if they say we have a chance of a fight, we need to get away as quickly as we can, sir."

"You're making no sense, Delius."

"Understood, sir," he replied as he clambered to his feet. "Thank you, sir. If you please, if I may, can I…?" As chance would have it, Swamsoot recognised this blind panic as something much too commonplace at home amongst his fellow military men and women. That Delius had decided to run away before completing the request to do so was to be expected. Swamsoot walked slowly back into the ship, gracefully side-stepping the fleeing hordes.

"Please, never allow an invasion," he motioned skyward. "Particularly from a tall race." By the time he found his way to the communications room, he was the one-man crew on a ship that housed hundreds and the life-form machines showed that even the unidentified stowaways had deserted along with his trusted soldiers. The whiz rod clicked quietly, with the new message lighting up the console in a variety of colours as the message repeated itself like a rainbow.

'Swamsoot, I have an idea. I believe you have a fighting chance. Message ends. Ethel Balldytireskid CPE.'

"Oh dear," he muttered softly. "They might not be back for days now that they've read that." Sitting down as heavily as a downtrodden husband after Christmas shopping, he began to construct a response without sounding too offensive or offended. He was a long way from home and as the crew would only come back when they were hungry, he couldn't afford to disenfranchise himself from the only friends he had.

"Ethel," he started sensibly. "Thanks for the news. Perhaps if you could forward all relevant information, I can put your plan into action as I am short of support here."

Diplomatic, he thought to himself and turned to find the empty vessel a little unnerving. Walls as clean and shining as these were a testament to the crew and their attention to cleaning detail was as detailed as their understanding and fear of anything from a flesh-eating reptilian giant to a small cat who can say boo. With limited options, the captain without a crew as he had become, decided to pay Tam a visit as if nothing had changed. Except now, he would be begging him to let him stay for the night. After all, it was dark and he was still a Bellsurpian. It wasn't until he moved away from the consoles that he noticed the Whiz Rod Port Connectors had been removed, presumably during the panic. It would mean messages would now take days to get back and forth to Bellsurp. He dredged up a human emotion as he headed towards the exit.

"Bugger."

Guess Who's Coming to Tam's

Tam approached his house with no little trepidation. Most of it looked the way it had looked for as long as he remembered, but for no obvious reason, it stuck out more at the back. For a man who had no relationship with the construction industry, the 'sticking out at the back' description seemed perfectly adequate and he walked crab-like to try and take in the full picture of what was unfolding before him. Inside, he heard Jack barking the way Jack always barked when somebody, anybody approached, which at least assured him he was at the right place.

Tam's house was a simple place with a small kitchen where he did all of his entertaining, which over the past few years had amounted to offering Swamsoot a drink. In addition to the kitchen and living room, he also had a 'posh lounge' which had remained under lock and key for as long as he could remember, just waiting for the right moment to show it off. It also housed a small utility room where Jack did his eating and sleeping, which used to be the bathroom. However, after watching a home improvement show on television, he converted the small bedroom into a bathroom and now made do with two bedrooms, one of which was as well used as a blind man's binoculars.

For no good reason now, though, he appeared to have a piece on the part of his house that faced the Groaty Mountain and the piece seemed to be bigger than the rest of his home. Walking sideways did nothing to clear up the mystery, so he decided to be brave and try the front door. At the very worst, this would afford him the knowledge of whether or not he had taken the wrong turn and was looking at a property similar to his but 'better'.

"Hello," he ventured as he pushed the door as gingerly as a ginger bread man pushing a ginger bread baby in its ginger bread pram.

"Woof," Jack answered, confident that his woof translated to 'hello'.

"Is that you, Jack?"

"Woof woof," answered Jack, confident that the translation meant, 'he's had one over the eight today'. Tam put his head around the door and switched on the light as the dusk began to steal parts of the daylight.

"Well, it's my kitchen." Jack lay down and refused to answer. Of all of the conversations he had shared with his master over the years, the ones fuelled by alcohol were always the most unpleasant, mainly due to the repetition.

"Who's my best boy?" Tam would ask.

"Woof," he'd say and then the whole drawn-out conversation would be repeated sixteen times until Jack eventually pretended he wanted to go out to chase whatever he could find. Tam was sober tonight, though and his odd behaviour would not include repetition towards his four-legged best friend but would be a selection of questions aimed at nobody in particular. Doing what any confused man would, Tam walked back out of his house for one last confirmation before investigating further. *Definitely mine,* he thought and so the inspection began in earnest. The kitchen table and matching furniture remained unchanged and everything in his favourite room appeared as it was when he left. Striding with as much confidence as he could, he opened the door to the 'posh lounge' to find a corridor leading away from the 'posh lounge' and past the utility room to another door which he couldn't remember opening in the years he had lived there. Things had taken a turn for the strange.

"Jack. Has anyone been here tonight with… another bit of a house?"

"Woof."

Striding was never going to be an option with this much unexplained, so a slow trudge ensued along a narrow corridor to the first of a number of doors. Doors that definitely weren't there before he left earlier that day.

"Should I knock, Jack?"

"Woof."

Oddly, he knocked. "Hello," he ventured as politely as any man could consider in his own home upon finding a secret passage. "Is there anyone there?"

"Woof!" Jack encouraged him.

"Do you think so, boy? Ok then, let's go in." Gleaming brass handles, too well polished to get his greasy hands on, he thought, adorned the oak-grained door, so he wiped his hands carefully on his shirt before turning them slowly. "Hello," he repeated. "It's me, Tam."

Poking his head around the door frame, he discovered a large, plainly decorated room twice the size of his posh lounge, though without furniture. Tam straightened up and walked calmly into the centre of the mysterious room and turned more circles than the night he was so drunk that he had his shoe nailed to the dance floor of the local parish hall. "Hello," he repeated with slightly less anxiety than a man who feels a bite when sitting on a toilet in the Australian outback. "Is there anyone here?"

The absence of noise like that is always deafening and Tam decided to try the next door, which led to a staircase in the general area where the back of his house once existed. *In for a penny*, he thought casually and strode manfully upwards without any real fear but with curiosity now taking a stranglehold on his senses. At the top of the stairs, he found a short hallway leading back to what he recognised as the rest of his first floor and three other doors, one leading to a bathroom and the others to two bedrooms, both neat and tidy but without furniture. After a few minutes of spinning and re-examining what he had found, a voice shouted from downstairs.

"Hello, Tam. Are you here, Tam?"

"Who's there?" he answered automatically, fully cognisant of the knowledge that it was Swamsoot on the ground floor of a bit of his building that he didn't have when he went out.

"It's me. Captain Damalgo Winstonian Swamsoot. I was wondering if I could perhaps… stay here tonight?"

Tam ran downstairs. "I've got more house than I had earlier. How do people get more house?"

"I've got less crew than I had earlier," Swamsoot replied with a hint of animosity. "And I couldn't quite figure that out either, but I managed to get to the bottom of it. I find that simple investigation determines outcome most times although there are times when it suits all parties to coordinate a series of sub-committees to attempt to…"

"I've got more house than I had when I left, son and I don't really know how that happened." Tam looked at Swamsoot and then back up the staircase before pointing like a man identifying the wasp who had just stung him for the wasp-sting police. "See that lot there? He implored the young-looking space traveller. "That wasn't there when I last looked. Mind you, I haven't been in this part of the house for some time, so it might be that I had just forgotten about it. Is that possible?"

"Yes," Swamsoot answered coldly. "Can I stay here tonight, please?"

"How can a piece of house that big go unnoticed, though? I'm not big on housekeeping. I've never denied that, but to lose a chunk…"

"As you have plenty of space, it seems reasonable to offer it to me on a short-term basis then, Tam."

Tam heard the question for the first time. "You want to stay here with me, son?"

"Yes, please. I'm afraid my crew have gone underground for the foreseeable future and it makes sense to not pursue in case I force them further into retreat." Tam looked quizzically at him. "It's a Bellsurpian trait."

"I see," Tam lied. "I don't think it's appropriate for a young feller to stay here with me without an adult, son."

Swamsoot scratched his head. "But you're an adult, aren't you?"

"I mean an adult that knows you."

"But you know me."

"Not very well, though, son."

"How well should you know someone before you allow them to sleep on a beach on a freezing, cold night with the elements and the wild dogs to pick away at them?"

"There are no wild dogs on Scroat, son, although there are a few people who eat and growl like wild animals, but they wouldn't eat you unless they are really hungry." The Bellsurpian cowardice appeared in Swamsoot's eyes for Tam to see. "I'm only joking, son," he explained quickly. "Half of the residents couldn't chew a slab of toffee, never mind a person."

Swamsoot brightened slightly. "May I stay here tonight?" he asked casually enough for the previous conversation to have never taken place. Tam looked at a scared youngster far away from home and tried to imagine how he would have coped in like-for-like conditions as a young man.

"Where's your crew then, although why you call them a crew is another little mystery to me?"

"Hiding."

"Left you all alone then?"

"Yes."

"And you feel a little apprehensive, then?"

Swamsoot scanned his in-built dictionary as deciphered by the mini translator in his pocket and found the word. "Apprehensive, yes."

"I'll have to ring Billy McJack and tell him. He's the local bobby and he'll have to OK it."

Swamsoot scanned. "Bobby?"

"Policeman."

"Ah, policeman. Can I stay?"

"I need to speak to Billy first."

"Billy, the bobby?"

"Aye."

Aye, Swamsoot thought. This has caused problems in the past, but as the Calistones weren't here to pick up on his panic, he inhaled deeply and pressed on.

"Aye?"

"Aye," Tam echoed. "Yes, it means yes. Aye means yes, son."

"Yes. Aye means yes," he repeated and smiled to himself, safe in the knowledge that a near tragedy could have been easily avoided by simply asking the right question. "I suppose yes means something else as well?"

Tam frowned as he picked up the telephone. "No," he answered with a sideways glance followed by an admonishing sniff. "Unless you're a woman, of course." Tam dialled quickly as Swamsoot scanned his electronic thesaurus.

"Mmm!" he mustered while Tam began to speak.

"That's just a joke in bad taste, son and I would appreciate it if you forget it. Agnes, it's Tam. How are you, sweetheart? Yes, I'll bring it round tomorrow morning if you need it. I know that, but most of the time, I cut too much off, especially if I have a drink before I cut it and then I'm too ashamed to come out of the house until it grows back to a reasonable length, but sorry to trouble you, Agnes. Is Billy back from the pub yet?"

Swamsoot assumed the obvious. "Would you like me to either cut or grow your hair?"

"Billy. I wasn't really expecting you to be home."

"Why did you ring me at home then, Tam?" he asked reasonably. After a confused pause, Tam continued.

"One of the kids has been stranded here and his mates have run away and left him. He wants to stay here for the night, but…" It seemed like an odd question, but Tam carried on talking. "I'm not sure he should be staying here with me if you know what I mean?"

"I'm not sure I do, actually, Tam. It's not as though he's going to come to any harm in your house, is he?"

"Well, no, but it is bigger than I remember it."

"Where are his mates then? I hope they stay away from the cliffs."

"That's a point." Tam interrupted, turning his attention back to a bored-looking Swamsoot. "They wouldn't go anywhere near the cliffs, would they?"

"Is there a risk of danger there?" asked the traveller purposefully.

"Of course there is."

"Then, no. They will not go anywhere near the cliffs."

"How do you know that?" asked the interested Scotsman.

"I know." Just as strangely, Tam believed him.

"They won't go anywhere near the cliffs, Billy."

"What do you mean, it's bigger than you remember it?"

"What is?" asked Tam.

"I don't know," Billy said, displaying a sense of confused mind. "You said it was bigger than you remember it, but you didn't say what was bigger than you remember it. So what is?"

"So what is what?"

"So what is bigger than you remember what?"

"What?"

"What?" A long pause settled over the old friends and Billy decided to take control of the situation as the officer of the constabulary should. "Listen, Tam. Let the kid stay there for tonight and make sure you find his teacher in the morning and give him a piece of your mind. In fact, don't give him a piece of your mind. You can't afford to lose any more of it." Before Tam could respond with a like-for-like insult, the line went dead and Tam was left alone with a strange young man who grinned contentedly as Tam spoke.

"Right then young… Tell me your name again, son?"

"Damalgo Winstonian Swamsoot."

"I see. And how old are you, son?"

"In your years, probably close to one hundred and eighty. Maybe more, maybe less." Tam scratched his head and Jack barked playfully before jumping on to Swamsoot's lap and settling down comfortably.

"One hundred and eighty?"

"Approximately one hundred and eighty, although from what I can gather, it could be a few years either way. Our timescales are very flexible back on Bellsurp."

"I see," Tam lied. "And I suppose your parents are over two hundred years old?"

"That is a very wise supposition, Tam, although they are probably over eight or nine hundred of your years. You'd never know it by looking at my Mother, though. Everyone says she looks like a three-hundred-year-old. Walks a lot, you see and drinks plenty of water."

Tam looked carefully at his guest and decided this was how kids behave these days. "I'm going to have another look at the rest of the house, then I'll make you a bite to eat. Do you like fish fingers?"

Swamsoot mused silently. "I suppose so. Do you like dog toes?"

Tam giggled through his response. "Very good. Dog toes. What about chicken's lips?" For some reason, he wasn't surprised when Swamsoot neither laughed or replied. "Well then, I'll go and check the house again and you can make yourself comfortable."

Swamsoot sat back and relaxed and soon he was drifting off into a peaceful, sleepy dream where all of his crew were well-educated, brave soldiers and the idea of inadvertently sending a scary message didn't create any cause for concern and all orders were carried out without nonsensical questions. Back in the days when he was training as a soldier, he had never been taught how the politically correct lobby would determine the makeup of a crew sent on what could be a vital mission to either save or destroy civilization and the dream was not interrupted by such considerations. As he dreamt back home on Bellsurp, two people were thinking seriously about how the mission to Earth was progressing and seemed close to a resolution.

"I think we've developed the perfect solution."

"So do I," answered General Battleprop. "Prepare the missiles and we'll destroy Earth while we have the chance."

Time Is of the Essence

Ethel stood up and marched swiftly across the room. Her attire was as simple as every clever person's ever was; a white coat hiding whatever else she wore and her bespectacled, tight-haired look was atypical of clever people the universe over.

"Why won't this water heater work?" she asked Bamber with a hint of frustration in her voice.

"It isn't turned on," he answered tersely. "And it's probably too tricky for a clever person to try unassisted. Why don't you just sit down and relax? My parents always told me that sitting down and relaxing would always produce a result, which is, I believe, precisely what we need now."

"The problem is," she answered caustically. "You've told me that little analogy before and unless I'm mistaken, it referred to constipation the last time."

Bamber gave a gormless grin and blushed. "Now you mention it…"

"We need a response from Swamsoot to tell us what he knows; otherwise, we're going to have to get down there after him. A fighting chance is only a fighting chance if we know he's able to fight." Bamber nodded in agreement before his thought process kicked in."

"Go down there after him?"

"I'd rather not have to, but if he doesn't respond soon, we may have little or no choice." It seemed a well-thought semi-idea, but at the bottom of his rough exterior Bamber was also a Bellsurpian and thus, the yellow stripe running the length of his back had only been punctured by opponent's weapons as he ran away from a fight.

"Let's just try a little harder to make contact, Ethel. After all, we wouldn't want to waste valuable time organising a crew, a vessel, a mission plan, as well as travel permits just to get there too late." Even though she was well aware of the Bellsurpian traits regarding cowardice, she assumed he was thinking practically, a rare and precious commodity amongst the military. A flick of the wrist later and the water heater was fired up and she was on her way back to the whiz rod to create another message.

"Are you going to mention the word 'fight' in this message?" he asked plainly, as he stood up and turned the heat down underneath the water before it caused an explosion. "Only, if you are, you should consider marking it for Damalgo's attention only. I'd hate to think what that word might do to the masses if they encounter it twice."

"Good point," she shouted with more animation than the answer required. "But I've just had another thought that might just mean they don't need to fight in any fashion whatsoever."

"Really?" asked Bamber, returning to his seat with a self-satisfied look safe in the knowledge that, as a clever person, Ethel was always going to produce a solution.

"Yes. How long in Earth time does it take to get a message to Earth?"

"How long in Earth moments does it take to get a ship to Earth?" asked Battleprop at the same moment in time.

"In Earth time, either ten minutes or about four days if the communications port is damaged or missing," answered Bamber Wetbot with his limited knowledge of that part of the universe.

"In Earth time, about four days," answered a minion that Battleprop had never met before to the same question.

"Right then," Ethel said confidently. "We could have them home safely within a few Earth days, four or five perhaps."

"Right then," Battleprop said confidently. "They could all be history within a few days. Four at the most, I'm thinking, should cover it."

And just to be ironic, Tam was busy throwing a blanket over Swamsoot and whispering. "That'll keep you warm. I don't want your mother ringing me because you've caught a cold."

Make a Decision, Then Stick By It

Only the inability to understand interplanetary time differences stood in the way of Swamsoot and his colleagues being annihilated. General Battleprop was widely regarded as a square-jawed genius when it came to dealing with the enemy, whoever the enemy may be, but he, like all military people, were viewed by the clever people as being no more than thick. Not that 'thick' was viewed as an insult by the military. In fact, the only way to insult the military on Bellsurp was to publicly question their ability to deal with personal matters.

From the days of the Government of Dalhag, when the threat of fear itself was all-consuming, came a new legislative body looking to popularise itself with the masses.

Every tree and lamp-post on Bellsurp was emblazoned with the poster of freedom (so-called because the Government of Dalhag deemed it popular to be free). Although most of the clever people didn't fall for the propaganda that the new leaders publicised, they were aware that it was new and, therefore, a threat to the cowards of Bellsurp. By default, it meant that the masses would follow it and as a result of those dark, confusing days, the military now coaxed people into their way of thinking by being nice.

Nice, that is in the way of smiling at the public as they told them anything, but as it was Bellsurp and a smile meant, usually, no punch in the nose was following, the public didn't really listen.

In the event that an attack was to be made on another planet, a public announcement had to be made and Battleprop prepared himself accordingly. Kissing the picture of Emperor Watswat, he began tuning his nasal passages with wild, rolling noises to make everyone aware he was about to speak and the minions did what all Bellsurpian minions did when Battleprop was about to speak. They hid.

Unperturbed, Battleprop moved to the press office in the corridor of Camp Bullwhip, where the cameras and microphones were prepared for his speech, where he settled into a huge, leather-like chair and waited for the automatic countdown. Large screens around the globe were interrupted by a robot.

"The following announcement is by General Battleprop of the great army of ancient Dalhag and will explain the need to attack and remove the threat of a distant star by the name of planet Earth."

Battleprop smiled and began confidently, "We are to attack and eliminate the threat of a distant star by the name of planet Earth."

"Transmission ends," said the robot.

Battleprop stood up and walked solemnly back to his office to prepare for war.

Back in her office, Ethel shook her head. "You have to admit. He has charisma."

"Do you think so?" Bamber asked genuinely. "To be honest, I think he's a bit rude and obnoxious, not to mention his body odour and lack of…"

"Bamber, I'm joking."

"But clever people don't know how to joke," he responded with just as much authenticity. "Particularly when it comes to matters of life and… the other thing. You know, the thing that's opposite to life."

"Death, Bamber. It's not necessarily a bad word, just so long as you don't try and inflict it on anyone. And before you tell me that's the job of a soldier, let me tell you that it isn't. The job of the soldier is to protect people around him and don't try thinking because soldiers aren't meant for thinking." Bamber recognised the minor insult but wasn't insulted by it.

"Ah!" he opened with by way of response. "If you recall, the only task Damalgo was given was to demonstrate that the people on Earth were stupid enough to buy anything, even if they don't want it, which in turn would demonstrate that they are so stupid that they present no threat. And he's a soldier." His tone suggested a feeling of superiority had overwhelmed him and he almost sneered.

"However," Ethel said with a tone of her own that already exuded sufficient confidence to blow his argument out of the water. "If he fails to sell them something that they don't want, they are to be annihilated. Unless I'm mistaken, that's your versions of the work of soldiers?"

Bamber mumbled softly, then decided that arguing with a clever person is an argument doomed to failure. "So, have you got a plan then?

"Yes," she answered. "I believe I do as it happens, but it means some smart work on our behalf and particularly on your behalf. I know you don't think you're capable of anything terribly clever, but I find that people are always at least capable of surprising themselves if the opportunity arises. So, if you're feeling up to it?"

Bamber paused momentarily before visibly perking up. "Sorry, I drifted off there. What did you say?"

Ethel looked at him and mused with great patience and, to great effect, before taking a deep breath and, without too much disguise, muttered, "Bugger."

Listen Carefully. I Will Say This Only Once

Tam was never classed as a romantic by anyone that knew him, but he loved to watch the sunrise over the calm horizon and rarely missed an opportunity to climb out of bed before the sun took off her pyjamas and showed herself for the first time in the mornings. Swamsoot shared a similar affection for the brightest part of the morning, but as he had a variety of sunrises to choose from every day, rising from his slumber was nowhere near as fraught with lack of selection.

In normal fashion, Tam slipped on his dressing gown without fastening it and walked slowly downstairs and into the kitchen. It wasn't every morning that he turned on the kettle and wondered if his house had really been extended to twice its size the previous night. In addition, it wasn't every morning he wondered where the youngster asleep on his settee came from and how he was going to get him back safely to where he had come from. As he spooned coffee into his favourite item of crockery that he hadn't seen washing up liquid for a year, Jack nuzzled softly against his bare leg.

"Hello, boy. Where did you sleep last night?" In time-honoured tradition, Jack wagged his tail and bared his teeth in one of those 'doesn't it look like he's smiling?' moments that dogs have to please their owners.

"Judging by the temperature and the hair on my legs," Swamsoot interjected, "I'd say on top of me."

"Ah," Tam sang out the way a trader does in a fish market. "Morning."

Traditions are what they are, Swamsoot thought. "Afternoon," he answered.'

"Coffee?" Tam asked logically.

"Brown and smelly," Swamsoot answered with his logic.

"Ah, your mother doesn't allow you to drink it yet, does she not?"

"Neither does yours then," he replied softly, his facial expression giving away his lack of confidence in social intercourse. "But if you want, I'll sell you some, although your mother doesn't let you use it for anything."

Tam duly ignored the babble and poured his own hot water. "There's fruit juice in the fridge if you want some," he said and picked up his cup before walking to the door with Jack hot on his trail. "But you had better get a spurt on because the big bulb is switching on in a minute and you don't want to miss that."

"You're absolutely correct, but by the same token, you don't want to miss the opportunity to purchase a selection of fine wines and cheeses that could be delivered to your door within forty-five working days if you give me your money now." And in the moment that he followed Tam out of the door, the Sun broke the early morning dusk with a little wink at the world and Swamsoot became strangely quietened by its beauty. "Oh," he muttered with the first touch of emotion since his arrival on Earth. "Now that is…"

"Beautiful," Tam answered without being asked and took a sip from his coffee before turning to the youngster. "Close your mouth, son. The flies will be getting out of bed soon. There's nothing to be ashamed of, by the way, because most people that see it for the first time find it reasonably astonishing. When I first came here about… actually, I was probably about the same age as you are now. What are you, fifteen or sixteen?"

Swamsoot pondered his response. "In Earth years, somewhere between one and two hundred, I suppose."

Tam wasn't listening. "And when I first saw it, I remember asking my dad if it was the moon saying goodnight or the sun saying good morning. Do you know what he said to me?" he asked, only half expecting a response of any description.

"Whilst I couldn't possibly know, I do know…"

"He said, don't be such a silly sod. Planets don't speak."

"That's not strictly true, of course, as the people on Chaltstonk insist that their hills and rivers speak every language…"

"He was the first full-time bobby on the island, as it happens and he wasn't given to romanticism of any sort, including the type my mother used to try on him. If ever a man wouldn't fall for a pitch from a woman, my dad was that man. I fancy I might have inherited that particular trait from him because I'm not big on falling for the bat of an eyelid or a sleek line from a smooth operator."

"What about falling for the need to collect money by simply paying for it up-front with the promise that you will get ten times the amount back?"

"It really is beautiful, isn't it?"

Swamsoot looked up at the sky and wondered where his crew was hiding and whether or not he would see them within the next day or two. More importantly, he wondered what he could do to get this Earth man to purchase something he didn't require, thus allowing him the opportunity to take word back to his superiors that they truly are so stupid that they pose no threat to any other race in the vicinity. Given that the vicinity the Bellsurpians referred to was ten thousand Earth years away with the current technology, the threat was about as dangerous as a snake rattling its tail from a sand bank in the equator at a careless child in Southampton. Swamsoot's bosses, however, were given caution on a bizarre scale and if this planet were a threat hundreds of years in the future, now would be a reasonable time to eradicate them.

It was a cross between extreme forward planning and the cowardice they were renowned for in equal measure. Worryingly, Swamsoot understood this position and was well aware that his returning crew or at least the Calistone contingent, would pick up on his worry vibe immediately, creating a second wave of panic which might result in crew disappearance for weeks or even months. His immediate thought was to search for them and return to Bellsurp under the failure banner and simply accept the criticism. Criticism, however, didn't sit comfortably in the Swamsoot house and he couldn't bear to be categorised along with Martin the Failure or Derek 'can't wipe his nose properly'. Winters.

Both men were roundly condemned for what most reasonable people called errors of judgement, although Derek was as messy as he was irresolute. Swamsoot needed to find someone to take advice from as his attempts to sell something useless and pointless were proving useless and pointless. In addition, he wasn't sure that Tam had such a high position in heraldry as he purported to have and selling uselessness to a useless person would hardly be considered a feather in the cap of a decorated soldier. Nonetheless, if he had no other obvious skill set, Swamsoot was a trier and the least he could do under the circumstances was try a little more.

"Tam," he opened tentatively. "Do you know why I'm here? I mean, why I'm actually here, in your home on the island of…"

"Scroat." Tam helped politely.

"Scroat, yes. Do you know why I'm here on the island of Scroat?"

Tam sipped his coffee. "Field trip?"

"No. I'm here to try and save the lives of millions of people from Scroat and other places across Earth. However, unless I can convince the people of Bellsurp that you pose no threat, I might have to simply climb aboard my ship and head off to leave you to your own devices. Do you understand?"

"Course I do," he lied.

"Well, do you suppose you could help me to help you?"

"I could do with a bit more milk in this. It's a little bit strong."

Swamsoot looked carefully at Tam and his automatic irony scan clicked in without success. The young-looking multi-centurion was uncomfortable in giving away the reason for his presence, but something inside him was aware that humans he had met were, by Bellsurpian standards, completely idiotic. No bad thing under the banner of his arrival, but sadly too stupid to listen to his sales pitch. Flying across time and space had given him ample opportunity to familiarise himself with selling power and the way of the TV executive. Surely all he had to do was inundate them with puerile, sardonic sales to have the whole race eating out of his hand. For some reason, though, this Tam character was oblivious to everything he tried. Scratching his chin thoughtfully, he made a more earnest attempt.

"I really need to make you aware of the impending danger facing you and your people, otherwise, you're going to be obliterated in a flash of power so extreme you can't imagine it in your worst dreams."

"So, can I have a drop more milk?"

"Can we forget about the milk just for a few moments, please?"

"Well, it's all well and good you wanting to forget about the milk, but I'm prone to mouth ulcers and if I get something hot *and* strong on one of those babies, then I make a bit of noise. And when I make noise, I really..."

"I'll get the milk," Swamsoot interrupted with a snort and a roll of the eyes that gave away a cross between frustration and apathy. "But all I want you to do is listen," he continued and as he waved his hand a half-empty milk bottle floated in from the kitchen. "And when I'm finished, you can complain all you want about your mouth ulcer if you think it's worthwhile. Deal?"

Tam watched carefully as the milk bottle made its way to his hand and he gently tipped it up and filled his cup with cold milk. The extension to his house was a mystery he was almost prepared to put down to alcohol-induced hallucination, but a flying milk bottle scared him a little.

"How do you do that then... what's your name again?"

"Swamsoot. Captain Swamsoot. Now, do I have your attention?"

Once More With No Feeling

Whilst a cat might be classed as curious, Ethel was an equivalent opposite when it came to men and the way their minds work or, for the sake of her stance, their refusal to do so. Bamber didn't necessarily engender confidence in anyone, but in a clever person's thought processes, confidence didn't come high in any event. Confidence tended to be classed alongside emotions and emotions only confused real thoughts. Clever people, however, were as confident as they could possibly be when it came to outfoxing the non-clevers, none of whom had any standing in the intellectual list on Bellsurp.

"Do you understand anything I've said so far?" she asked him plainly.

"It's hard to say, really, not least of all because my mind is still a bit busy thinking of a way to try and save Damalgo."

Ethel threw her hands in the air. "What do you think I've been talking about since we came in here?" Bamber noticed her nose twitch and thought of a small, long-eared creature he had once seen on a documentary made on a planet far away. Determined concentration didn't come high on his list of priorities and distractions were never far behind the beginning of any conversation.

"Is that a new screen?" he asked as he scratched himself in a place better reserved for the bathtub.

"Bamber. I think perhaps I should make myself clear in terms that even you can understand."

"OK"

"OK? Is that it? Right. OK. In that case," she went on as the average room temperature rose along with her cheeks. "It's nice and simple, really. You need to take a small crew and fly to Earth, making sure you arrive before the next warship gets there, which means you have very little time to find a crew, train a crew and brief a crew." More than a moment passed as they stared into each other's eyes.

"Brief a crew? With what brief?"

"Well, in basic stipulations and provisos, you need to tell them nothing to ensure you can't compromise the mission."

"I see," he lied.

"When I say compromise the mission, do you understand to what I am referring?"

"Basically."

"How, basically?"

"Very basically."

"Do you understand any of it?"

"No."

Ethel swallowed hard and squeezed a grin out of lips tight enough to crush gravel.

Say It Again. Just Once

Ethel had sent the second message immediately after the first, explaining that the phrase 'fighting chance' did not mean there was a chance of a fight, but it wasn't read. Of course, it wasn't read. *What could she have bene thinking about?* The second message arrived on a screen on an empty vessel and the third message was very specific and directed very specifically to Damalgo Winstonian Swamsoot;

Dearest Damalgo. I have tried to convince the military to give you all of the time you need to convince the daft Earthlings to buy some unnecessary product, but they are loathe to bend. After lengthy debates and arguments and debates from both sides, it has been agreed that they will be firing Stingwow missiles in one human day, which will allow you four human days to get off the planet before it is annihilated.

Yours truly,

Ethel.

PS-don't forget to bring a gift for the king. He likes soft toys.

Damalgo Winstonian Swamsoot, however, was busy trying to cope with the reality that his target, one Tam

Wilson, did not seem to want anything that he didn't need. Further to that, his crew had deserted and were unlikely to be seen for at least half a day as the chances of them staying outdoors in the dark were slim. By default, this meant he did not receive the message from his staff, nor did he receive the follow-up message, which read;

Just noticed your readouts show your equipment is damaged, which means that the Stingwow missiles will now move quicker than radio waves and Earth will probably be expunged before you get this message.

Without him knowing, things had taken a turn for the scary!

Any News

Jack knew when his first walk of the day was, the way all dogs do and Jack's was the same every day, when Tam could be bothered.

"Come on, Jack. We'll go and get some milk. That flying stuff must be off."

"Are you sure you need milk, Tam? Perhaps you can get some just because I asked you to?"

"Ok, son. You can tell people that if you want to." Swamsoot stared deeply at the rugged Scot, but without the devices to test for irony or a portable Calistone, he just didn't possess the skill-set to detect sarcasm.

"Tell you what, Tam. I'll pop back to the craft and see what… I'll go and see what we have to… I'll…" But Tam had already walked off.

"As you wish, son. I'll maybe see you later if you don't find your teacher and your friends."

"Tam. Jack has gone the other way."

"Aye, into the bushes. We don't pick it up in the countryside."

"What? You don't pick what up?" Tam wandered away with a dismissive wave as Swamsoot walked quickly back to the craft, which had brought them much further than any human could possibly imagine. He climbed on board the craft with so many advancements that the most advanced of the human species would barely be able to activate the light switches. He touched his computer screen and gave a little humming noise to stimulate the voice recognition and carefully read the lack of messages from Ethel Balldytireskid and allowed himself one syllable by way of reaction. "Pooh!"

Things Seem a Little Odd

When Tam arrived at the shop, he told Jack to wait, safe in the knowledge that he wouldn't wait and tutted at the arrival bell that twanged above the old timber door as he entered the local shop/library/police station. Gracie Chapple stood solemnly behind the counter, unsure if she was serving the island's grumpiest man with a summons, A Tale of two Cities, a loaf of bread or just an argument to keep himself ticking over.

"What can I do for you today, Tam?" she asked bitterly.

"Milk and bread, please, Gracie. Have you seen any of the kids from the trip?"

"Trip?"

"Aye, the school trip. One of them got stuck at my place last night and I think he was a bit scared."

"Who would blame the poor mite, being stuck with on auld goat like you? What did you do to make him scared?"

"Nothing. I came back from the pub and he was there to tell me that he couldn't find any of his pals and could he stay at my place on the cliff."

"Well, I didn't even know there was a trip on the island, but why should I know anything that goes on here, only being the nearest thing to a police officer?"

"Being Billy's sister hardly qualifies you as a police officer, Gracie, although you've probably been in more fights."

"That may be true, Tam Wilson, but I would still expect him to let me know when we're going to be overrun by a group of children, especially if they're going to be swarming in here with their little spindly fingers helping themselves to my goodies."

"Goodies? I don't think Syrup-of-Date classes as goodies these days, Gracie or indeed, whether it ever did. Milk and bread on the slate, please? And I'll take a bottle of pop in case the kids turn up again."

"Ok, Tam. Have a nice day and stay sober."

"Aye, and you stay pretty."

"Cheeky bugger."

"By the way, Gracie. You've been to my place plenty of times."

"That was a different time, Tam when we were both lonely and a little…"

"I don't mean that. I just want to ask if you remember the lay-out of my place."

"There's really not much to remember, is there? Unless you've had it extended since I was last there?"

"Aye, that's what I thought. Bye Gracie."

Tam stepped outside and whistled for Jack, who was nowhere to be seen, although he would catch Tam long before he made it to the cliff-edge path and would undoubtedly be carrying some treat in his mouth that Tam wouldn't ask about. The confused islander started walking a little slower than his usual snails-pace as he pondered out loud, "How can I possibly have an extension on my house, which is bigger than my house, that wasn't there last night and how can a milk bottle float?" Just then, Jack ran past him carrying a whole chicken.

Keep It to Yourself

Swamsoot looked at the messages that Ethel had originally sent and pretended he didn't care that she hadn't ended any of them with a kiss. Moreover, he wondered how he could convince Tam to buy something he didn't want or need and for the first time that he could remember, he wished some of his officers would come back, not necessarily to take advice, but he always felt vindicated when he had someone to explain what he wasn't sure about.

Lights flashed on the console before him and he decided his best form of communication would be to send a suggestion back to the clever people of Bellsurp millions of miles away to people who couldn't possibly have any bearing on the outcome, such was the delay due to the unfathomable distance between the two planets.

Message: *Decided I will give King? Tam one last chance but will have to explain the danger that he and his subjects will be in. Will explain he has one chance to succumb to the will of the Bellsurpian High Command of he will face obliteration.*

Swamsoot read it back and decided the word *will* appeared too often but left it anyway as a sign of rebellion against his language teachers back home. Language teachers on Bellsurp were largely viewed through squinted eyes and usually smelt of biscuits, so the freedom to make them angry from such a distance was oddly satisfying.

Language teachers also had the terrifying knack of being able to drift in and out of perceptibility as they were thin enough to periodically become invisible. Supported by a gene that supported the invisibility when they became agitated potentially made them warriors to be feared in the land where anything to be feared was petrifying. As Bellsurpians, however, they were terrified of their own ability, so they made careers out of telling people how to speak.

Musing on his school days, he smiled maliciously and pressed the send button before going back to meet Tam and explain how he and the rest of planet Earth could well be blown to fifteen corners of the universe if they didn't play ball. The message would take four Earth days to arrive, whereupon a decision would be taken to either criticise or support the young travelling skipper. Had he waited another ten Earth minutes, he would have received the message from the military leaders who had circumvented the technology and the clever people and forwarded their own message, which read;

Have decided to obliterate Earth. Missiles travel quicker than messages. When you read this, you will have approximately twelve Earth hours to get off the planet or you will be vaporised with your hosts. Enjoy your tea!

Swamsoot walked towards Tam's house, unaware that if that message found its way to his crew, they would leave with or without him. Thankfully, they were all hiding in trees.

Oh the Irony

"Can I come in?" Swamsoot knocked and shouted when he arrived at Tam's house. Tam, however, was still meandering back towards his home with bread and milk and a well-fed Jack Russel who, in every sense of the word, was spitting feathers. The young Bellsurpian let himself into the empty house and waited patiently until they arrived home.

He flicked through the pages of the magazines scattered on the seats and was slightly confused by the number of articles on cars. The roads on Scroat appeared to number just one that ran through the village and the number of cars was considerably less than the number of people. During the journey to Earth, he had watched a couple of Steve McQueen movies and understood the relationship to automobiles that the male of the species seemed to appreciate. A flicker of light entered his mind.

"Cars. That's it. Cars."

"What about cars?" asked Tam as Jack ran past him in a strange show of excitement upon seeing him after only a couple of hours.

"Hello, Tam. Jack seems to be a bit... feathery and a bit... greasy."

"Aye, he stole a chicken. So, what about cars?"

Swamsoot immediately went on the offensive. "Do you need a car when you live here?"

"My God, no. You couldn't get your Ferrari into second gear on this island. Why do you ask?"

"So, you don't need one, but would you like to buy one?"

"Ha ha, yes, I'd love one and I don't know any real man who wouldn't want a Ferrari on his drive." he laughed as he put the milk in the fridge. "Do you want a drink of something, son? I have pop. No flying milk, though."

"No, thank you, but if you want to buy a Ferrari, then I might have a drink?"

"If I could buy a Ferrari, I would be living on a yacht and only coming on shore to cruise along the Amalfi Coast or through the winding roads of Monaco."

"Really?" asked Swamsoot, suddenly intrigued by the development. "What makes those places better than Scroat?"

"What makes *those* places better than Scroat? How much time do you have, son?"

Swamsoot smiled unapologetically. "All the time in the world," he answered as the missiles were fired from his neighbouring village of Grantiswat.

Don't Look Ethel

Roughly eight hundred yards away, a rustling was heard up a tree, followed by some mumbling, flatulence and giggling, then what appeared to be a muffled argument and eventually the sound of shushing. The silence that followed was eventually broken when a sleeping Calistone fell out of the tree and woke to find himself seemingly alone.

"Hello," he ventured. "Is there anyone here?"

"No," came the answer.

"So, where are you?"

"We're all up the tree."

"I see," he replied cautiously. "There doesn't appear to be anyone down here to be afraid of."

"Look more carefully."

This he did. "Yeah, there's not really anyone anywhere, so far as I can see. What do you suppose these fighters look like?" That gave way to various voices.

"I heard they're about twenty feet tall."

"With three heads."

"And red and blue teeth."

"And when they bite you, it makes you go red and blue."

"And then you explode."

"And they eat what's left of you."

"And if they don't like the way you taste, they feed you to the little hairy humans with all of the legs."

"Hang on a bit," Delius intervened from the dense foliage full of dense soldiers. "Where did you lot hear all of these things?"

The silence was only broken by the sounds of sliding down trees and the general moaning of big babies scratching themselves on the bark of trees. As they stood around in a general malaise, Delius decided to take the reins and steer the crew back to the waiting landing craft.

"Right, men, Calistones and whatever else we have. Sorry if I missed you out there, but I would really need the attendance register to remind myself who we brought." A general nod and a reluctant acceptance later, they had all started walking back towards the landing craft very gingerly. Delius would take the register, account for everyone, including stowaways and would set them all tasks to ensure the safe management of their ship before their beloved Captain Swamsoot returned. Suddenly the world seemed a better and less scary place as long as nobody looked at the computer screens or read any of the messages from Bellsurp. Delius sat down in front of his screen and gave a little gasp.

Its Only Business

"Ok, Tam. As you don't need one, why don't you buy a Ferrari today?"

"Good question. Do you want a drink of pop?"

"No, thank you, but will you buy a Ferrari?"

"No, but will you have a drink of pop?"

"But you said you would love one."

"And all kids are supposed to love pop."

"I'm not a kid," he moaned like a kid.

"Ok then, all young men love pop. Have a drink of pop."

Swamsoot mused, then spoke with inspiration. "If I drink some pop, will you buy a Ferrari?"

Tam snorted once. "It's a deal," he said and unscrewed the chunky top from the heavy bottle and proceeded to pour a large tumbler for his guest, who showed precious little by way of interest. Drinking deeply and grudgingly, he placed the glass on the table and spoke gravely.

"You will now buy a Ferrari, please."

"Well," Tam started with assurance. "Two things that make it difficult. One is that you don't have a Ferrari to sell and two, I don't have about one-hundred-and-fifty-thousand pounds to buy one with."

"Mmmm. Ok. Ok. I've seen this done on QVC. I'm not asking for one-hundred-and-fifty-thousand pounds. I'm asking for… What's a reasonable sum to pay for a Ferrari…" He looked at the picture in the magazine. "458?"

"Well, with my bank account, about fifteen pounds is all I can stretch to."

"Sold!" Swamsoot shouted. "And the world lives on. All you need to do is give me the fifteen pounds and I will go and get your Ferrari 458." He picked up the magazine and left the house via the front door. The noise and following flash didn't seem excessive to Tam, although he had no idea what it was. When the young traveller returned, he carried a set of keys, an invoice and a receipt book. "Your vehicle is outside the front door, sir and that will be fifteen pounds for something you definitely don't need."

"Oh, right," Tam replied with obvious disinterest.

"Fifteen pounds, please, sir?"

"Ok, will you take a cheque?" he asked reluctantly, playing along.

"Of course, sir. Your credit is good on this island."

Tam smiled. He hadn't heard that phrase for many years. "Ok, my cheque book is… actually, you know what? I have no idea where my cheque book is. Isn't that weird? I honestly can't remember when I last signed a cheque."

"No matter, sir. If you sign this invoice, I will ensure the relevant agencies are made aware of the transaction." Tam agreed to sign to placate the now-too-tired joke and took a set of keys from Swamsoot as he walked to the door. "Well, Tam. It's been a real pleasure meeting you and I hope you will continue to rule over your underlings with compassion and bravery in equal measure and that your dark nights are kept at bay by a child light. Goodbye, Tam." With that, he left the house and Tam followed him through the door where a gleaming red Ferrari 458 sat on his drive. The confused Scot stared at the car, then at the keys, followed by the invoice and receipt in his hands before looking up to see Swamsoot marching triumphantly towards his spaceship, which had taken off for home five minutes earlier and left him stranded on a doomed planet.

Pay Attention

"This is a pickle," Swamsoot noted wryly. "What I need here is some assurance that nobody has turned up and stolen the vessel or… Actually, that's pretty much all I can hope that hasn't happened. Does that make sense?" Even Bellsurpians allowed themselves countenance under stressful situations and as he was alone, he produced a cross between a sneer and a snort before deciding to go back to ask Tam if he had seen his spaceship. As he rounded the corner, he heard the roar of the engine on the Ferrari as it sped off into the distance and he felt physically sick that the only person he knew had just deserted him. Soft grass, still slightly damp from the early morning dew, softened the impact as he dropped to his knees after staring emptily for a full minute.

"Noooooooooo!" he wailed with passion, then brightened as the Ferrari reappeared behind him, having completed one full lap of the island road. Tam climbed out of the car and waved to Swamsoot before lifting jack out, closing the door and smiling at the perfect click the door made as it shut softly into the frame.

"This is beautiful," he shouted to his new friend as he approached. "And I don't care how long I have it for; it's already the most fun I've ever had."

"I have a problem, Tam."

"Ah," he replied with an air of acceptance. "Your dad wants it back already? You can tell him I only took it for a spin around the cliff edge and down to Spoor Duck View and it's as immaculate as it was when you dropped it off."

"My crew has deserted me. Tam and I seem to be stuck on your planet, although they won't know that until they climb out of wherever they're hiding. It appears that my vessel has been stolen. I must say that is confusing within itself as nobody on this planet is smart enough to manage any of the fundamentals required to direct anything vaguely interplanetary. Mmm."

"She is magnificent in the turns; fast and assured and very flat at speed. Everything I ever expected, I suppose. Your dad is a very lucky man."

"He is. He won the first six colours of Cryandow 15 when they were brought from the Grey Moon of Tramdahore. He always claimed he knew exactly what the code was, but my mother maintained he had sipped Catpaw before he went to bed that night and had an illegal dream that gave him the answers."

Tam stared, then continued, "Much more comfortable than I expected as well. For some reason, I thought it would be like sliding downhill on a skate and Beano annual, but no, it was really comfy and easy to handle."

Swamsoot stared with no little menace but utilised his military training to ease the pressure he was feeling. "Tam, can I ask you to sit down, please? I need to tell you what I didn't want to tell you but then thought I would have to tell you then eventually didn't need to mention because you made it easy for me to tell you nothing about what the clever people would class as something I shouldn't have told you about."

Tam took a guess at the response. "Ok!"

Remain Loyal at All Cost

Some considerable distance away and some considerable time ago, the countdown had started and passed without incident and the missiles were on the way. Ethel had only just been told about the imminent destruction of the planet with the would-be love of her life ensconced therein and she rushed to find Bamber to try something, anything that would ensure his safe removal of what was soon-to-be dust particles spread across dark space.

"How can we get a message to him, Bamber?

"If he was within distance we could get one of the Higher Calistones to send telepathic thoughts to the other Calistones, but he's just too far away. I'm sure he'll be fine, though and I will be very surprised if he isn't already on the way home with a success story to be told about how he managed to convince the Earthlings to succumb to his charm and wit."

"But if he's already done that, what's the point of destroying the place? Isn't that the whole mission purpose?"

"Well, when you put it that way, you could certainly make an argument for…"

"For what? For not killing billions of Earthlings and whatever other creatures exist down there?"

"Yes, that's one of the things you could say and that would be all right."

"All right? What do you mean, all right? Apart from everyone on that planet, your best friend might still be there, stranded and waiting just to be blown up by our military geniuses who are incapable of any form of social interaction within their own species, never mind trying to communicate with someone slightly different."

"Steady on, Ethel. Just because you and your friends have brains, the size of the stars doesn't mean we aren't as clever as you."

Ethel took in a deep breath and wiped the sweat off her top lip. "That is exactly what it means and that is exactly why we are here, to advise people like the military not to make ridiculous decisions without knowing what the consequences are. They haven't even checked to see if Damalgo's ship is airborne and whether or not life forms are registering."

"Well, I can do that, but like I said earlier, don't worry about that because if there's a couple of things I know about this mission, it is that Damalgo Winstonian Swamsoot is as good as any captain in the whole star fleet and his crew are as reliable and loyal as any crew ever assembled.

Millions of miles away from both planets, Delius had taken control of the ship and was busy saying a few words in front of the plaque that had been created in memory of their former leader.

A Failure to Communicate

"Here's the deal, Tam. My ship has gone missing, which means, I think, that I now live with you."

"I see."

"And on top of thar, my crew will want to live with you too, as-and-when they come out of hiding."

"I see."

"And I'm not really sure how many people that amounts to as we have Calistones and stowaways."

"A can of Stones?"

"Calistones, but they're not too much trouble even when they try and read your mind, which they do most commonly when you're asleep because they love to know what people dream about and if you're having a… you know… a dream that you shouldn't be having, then they tend to giggle and wake you up."

"I see."

"But they have a remarkable skill for not taking up any space and you'd wonder where they get to, which explains why they're so good at hiding as well, of course, otherwise I'd be out searching for them now, but they can hide better than I can search."

"I see."

"So, here's the whole deal, Tam. I managed to sell you the Ferrari for the money you didn't have for a car you don't want, so that is a clear demonstration of subjugation which will satisfy the leaders back home. That means you no longer present a threat to the universe because we could send someone with the simplest of mind control techniques to overthrow great rulers like you without any threat being made. It also keeps the clever people happy because they always argue that we should be trying to befriend other planets rather than blow them to smithereens."

"I see. Are you following this, Jack?" Tam asked pleasantly.

"Woof!"

"He understands."

"Yes, I heard him. So the bottom line is that the clever people will alert the military people and they, in turn, will advise our leaders and this mission will be declared a huge success and..."

"I see."

"No. I haven't finished."

"I see."

You see what?"

"Whatever it is you're talking about. Can we just talk about the Ferrari for a moment?"

"But I've just realised something. The message needs to be sent from the ship. I have a mobile danatron but need an interpretive antennae. I don't have one. I did see something in your bedroom that I may be able to use. Mmmm. If the landing craft has been stolen and the crew are all missing, then we have no way of getting the message of gloatery back to Bellsurp, which means they don't know how dim you are; therefore, they will still see you as a threat."

"So, the Ferrari?"

"Hang on, Tam. I need to go and check a few things, but before I do, would you be very upset if the message I was hoping to send can't be sent and it results in the destruction of your planet and everything on it?"

Tam thought momentarily. "Not your fault, is it?"

"Mmmm." Swamsoot offered and walked out into the sunshine to look for his crew, who were so far out of range that nothing on Earth was advanced enough to make contact with them.

If You Stand on One Leg and Vibrate Slightly

Fret was an unknown phenomenon on Bellsurp and Swamsoot was slightly confused by the repeated need to wipe his cheeks dry. Oceans and seas at home were largely non-tidal and dry, so when the wind was ordered to whip up a storm, it was done as an aid to electricity production, but because Bellsurpians were scared of that, they always stayed indoors during bouts of the airstream.

As he stood on the cliff edge path watching the waves roll towards Scroat from the North Atlantic, he frantically fiddled with the antenna on his danatron phone to try and pick up a stray signal from one of his crew that would give him a hint to their whereabouts and hopefully allow him to confirm the vital communication had been made. For the first time in this mission, the young skipper started to worry about what might not have happened. There was a considerable list of things that had happened that disturbed him and most of his allotted administrative time was spent sending memos condemning those crew members responsible for transgressions mainly linked to delinquent behaviour. Suddenly and unavoidably, he now needed to get appropriate messages to them in the hope that he could start a memo with.

'To whoever did this, well done etc', as opposed to the much more frequent version of 'To whoever did this, I will find you and tear your arms off', which always identified the transgressor by way of them hiding and missing shifts from the roster. Bellsurpian ways were functional when it came to flushing out cowards, but alas, as he was about to find out when they decided to hide, they are as good as anyone in the known, or for that matter, the unknown universe.

When they had decided to flee without informing him, though, what he wasn't aware of was that his associate's hiding ability was the least of his worries. The crew and the missiles would pass each other going in opposite directions in about four hours and Swamsoot was trying to find them with a phone and a coat hanger.

I Can See You. No, You Can't

Two long hours passed on board and Delius had yet to submit any kind of orders to his newly acquired crew and his attempts to not panic was proving difficult. Each time one of the Calistones moved within thinking distance, Delius tried to send his own mind into passive lock-down, thus sending the mind readers into empty thought processes and avoiding the need to drift towards terror-laden thoughts. Unfortunately, Calistones have an in-built suspicion gene which recognises excess empty-headedness and inevitably dread soon followed as the craft went into 'shelter first' mode, a system devised by Glandular Remedy, one of the planet's greatest ever warriors who was faced with enormous numbers during a historical conflict and decided to hide under the ship's console.

The enemy boarded his craft, but as they were very tall, never found him cowering under his desk in the dark. Instant hero-worship was bestowed upon him and his system became the staple for all fighting forces and running away forces alike. Within a very short period of time, the craft and all of its occupants were in 'shelter first' mode and drifting towards home when a rogue, highly unlikely signal from Swamsoot's mobile device flashed momentarily across the screen, which read. *Delius. Wherever you are, come and get me. Your perfect leader. Damalgo Winstonian Swamso.* Because the device message service only allowed 71 characters plus punctuation, he couldn't complete his name. Because Delius was hiding with the rest of the crew, he missed it. Back on Earth, Swamsoot was starting to worry, unaware that his worrying was going undetected.

Deep Breaths

Tam was somehow unsurprised when he came back to the house and was somehow unsurprised when he told him he couldn't find his friends.

"Do you want a drink of pop, son?"

"No, thank you. What I need is to find my crew and save you and your planet."

"Pop always makes kids…sorry, always makes young men feel better about themselves, so why not have a glass."

Swamsoot sat down heavily and thought long and hard about what he was dealing with, even taking into account the oath that he signed after qualifying at pilot school. The school coat of arms proudly displayed the motto; Emplurobo Escoorobo Daftoolobro. The simple translation was *Keep secrets, Don't tell fibs and Stop messing about*. It was the basis of the Bellsurpian flyers bible and he felt as though he was about to betray the very sentiment by telling Tam everything, although he had already divulged more than he should have done. On the basis that the ship was gone and obliteration was around the corner, he went for the oft-used adage of 'meh, why not' and asked Tam to buckle in.

The Genius of Stupidity

Most of the star fleets ships were new in as much as the biggest crime on the whole planet was scrap collection and every time a ship was parked, it was likely to be stripped by the time its pilot had returned with a sandwich. This meant a healthy industry line for starship construction and as most constructors had a sideline in scrap metal collection, the profession kept rolling on happily. In addition, new technology guaranteed upgrades with virtually every vessel, so individuals employed by the Institute Of Clever People also made hay when the suns shone.

Ethel pawed over the blueprints of Swamsoot's ship, frantically searching for something, anything that would allow her to affect the running or operation enough to at least have him register concern and flee. She was, of course, relying on Bellsurpian courage to make him jump in his vessel and head for the stars, but what she couldn't be aware of was that his crew had beaten him to it by displaying the levels of their own courage.

Reams of paper were strewn across her desk and she repeatedly growled at Dorian Gooray for not being more helpful in her search. Dorian was a renowned youth technician who was mainly notorious for his time spent looking at himself in anything shiny, but he was very talented when it came to the type of detail that bored everyone else.

"What's this?" she demanded as she scoured the first document.

"It's the back of the danatron," he answered methodically.

"What's this?" she asked, pointing to something an inch away.

"It's the back of the danatron."

"But you said that was the back of the danatron."

"It is, but so is that because you're pointing at the same thing, just further down the page." Ethel resisted the temptation to slap his arrogant face and besides, he had turned his arrogant face away from her to catch a sideways glance in the office window.

"What's this" she pointed extravagantly.

"It's the dead-mans-handle" he answered, scarcely moving his gaze from his own reflection.

"Why do we still have those things? They're archaic."

Dorian momentarily looked at her. "According to the mechanical weezer..."

"The robot?"

"Yes, according to the robot, we still need them in case our pilots fall asleep at the helm and fly one of our craft into something harder than the craft."

"So we take orders from a robot when we build space crafts?"

"No, sir, miss, ma'am, boss. The information tells us we need them as a safety device only but when they were briefing the pilots at the appraisal meeting, most of them fell asleep so it was deemed essential because of the fondness for kip."

"Mmm," she mumbled. "Waste of time and money, if you ask me. What's this?"

"It's the back of the danatron," he answered, then screamed as she slapped him.

Many miles away, a stroke of luck was happening in her favour, which she would never find out. Delius had walked into the cockpit and noticed a coat draped on one of the consoles.

"Who does this belong to?" he demanded with enough authority to fool the subordinates into believing he knew anything about the function of the ship. Naturally, the tone was enough to ensure nobody was brave enough to own up. He walked slowly towards it to notice the words clearly written in large, white square-text letters. 'DEAD MANS HAND'. On this occasion, the coat hid enough to create an emotion obviously identified as panic by the nearest Calistones.

"I sense fear," came a nearby voice.

"No, it's not…" Delius started, but it was too late and like a giant snowball rolling through the vast corridors of his command, the terror spread. As a newly ordained commander, he considered trying to fix it but instead dived for a space under the desk and fed off the panic vibes that everyone else was being subjected to. Just then, the dead-mans-handle console started flashing to wake up any on-duty sleepers and when he popped his head up to see the commotion, he was faced with a flashing red 'DEAD MANS HAND'. Delius was not a fool. He was nowhere near as clever as a fool, but he knew a sign when he saw one and a message telling him that they had their dead leader's hand became too much for his guilt complex.

"We're going back for him. Glory to Bellsurp," he screamed.

"Bravo!" came the response from a singular distant voice and within an instant, the ship was spun like a wasp attached to a hair and they were heading back the way they came.

Unknown to him, the missiles had just passed them by and were perilously close to Earth.

Something Awful Is Coming for Tea

Tam sat quietly with a cup of tea and a Jack Russel while Swamsoot laid it out.

"Did you notice the extra bit of house on your house?"

"Actually, yes, I did," he answered as he sipped the hot tea. "I mentioned that, didn't I Jack?"

"Woof!"

"Well, nobody on Earth has the technology to do that as quickly and precisely, although we did inadvertently send you the detail some years ago when we were observing and sent the digital printer."

"Digital printer?"

"Yes, and we do basically the same with everything nowadays except living tissue. That's how you got your Ferrari; by me looking at a photograph, then feeding it through the printer and giving you a replica. Our photography is a tad more advanced than yours, so we get to see the mechanics of these things. Buildings are easy."

"I see," Tam answered without honesty.

"So when you come from a planet that is so far advanced to yours, we can probably reasonably make demands of you and as our team of observers has identified you as being a bit thick, the decision to control you rather than kill you was agreed."

"I'm pleased to hear it," Tam said, unaware of his own sarcasm.

"Good," Swamsoot responded, just as unaware. "So all we need to do is get a message back to my planet so we can..."

"Can I stop you there for a minute, son?"

"As long as it's not to ask if I want a drink of pop."

"This thing with the house and the Ferrari. It's not that I don't believe you, it's just that... I don't believe what you're telling me. Does that sound better?"

"Better than what?"

"Better than me just calling you a liar?"

Swamsoot pondered for a moment. "Come with me, Tam," he said and set off for the front door with man and dog on his trail. "What about an Aston Martin? I watched a James Bond film on the way here and they look nice." Tam and Jack followed but didn't respond verbally, although the human shrug was noticeably indifferent.

"As you would probably say, they're nice enough."

Swamsoot took out a small device, pressed a few buttons and stepped back as an Aston Martin DB9 appeared next to the Ferrari.

"Like I would say, they're *definitely* nice enough. Now there's nothing on Earth capable of doing that, is there?"

"Well…"

"Of course, there's not, but you do have a telescope that can send a message a long way called Hubble and if you can get me to it, I can send a message to my people to make sure they don't obliterate you and that the mission has been a success. Can you do that?"

"Do what?"

"Get me to Hubble?"

"Where the hell is Hubble?"

"I don't know," implored the increasingly frustrated pilot. "It's your planet and you must know where everything is and if not, you can get one of your minions to take me there. What about one of the dolts in the village?"

"Oh aye, that's a good way to get a favour; call them names."

"What do you mean, a favour? Telling your subjects what to do isn't asking for a favour. It's telling them what to do."

"And what do you mean, my onions?"

"Minions, not onions."

"I don't have any minions. I don't have any onions either now. I come to think of it. I think I'll have liver and onions for my tea tonight. I always cook them in different pans, though, because the onions aren't good for Jack and I also put…"

"I really don't care about how you cook your onions, Tam," interrupted Swamsoot with some considerable emotion. "There's a good chance my military colleagues are plotting to send missiles here to blow your planet up and everyone on it, so I need you to get me to Hubble and as you're the most important person on Earth, I'm guessing you can get me there?"

The lengthy pause was deafening.

"Let me make a call." Tam walked to his hallway occasional table where an old-fashioned red telephone sat proudly amongst a litter bin's worth of scribbled notes and dialled a number. "Eddie, it's Tam. Aye, I'm ok. No, there's nothing wrong. Why shouldn't I phone you in the middle of the day? Would you be happier if I rang you in the middle of the night, you old fool? Aye, and the same to you," and with that, he slammed the receiver down. Naturally, it wasn't until he looked at Swamsoot did he realise the error of his ways and redialled the same number. "Eddie, it's Tam. Aye, I'm ok, but listen; you keep an eye on world events, don't you? Can you tell me where Hubble is? I think so. I'll just check." He turned back to his listening visitor. "Do you mean the Hubble telescope?"

"Yes, of course, I do," he snapped

"Aye, the Hubble telescope. Do you know where it is? Really? That high? How does anyone look through that, then? Really? Ok, thanks, Eddie. I'll see you at Milly's tonight. Aye and bring your wallet."

"Well?"

"It's in space, apparently."

"What?"

"It's hovering in space and you need a computer to look through it."

"I don't want to look through it. I want to send a virtual message through it."

"Don't know how you do that, but it's still in space. Space is up there," he said, pointing upwards and without irony. "Where the sky and the stars and… is that really where you're from? Are you really a Martian?"

"Of course, I'm not a Martian. I'm a Bellsurpian and proud of it and more importantly, Tam is that I hoped this mission would allow me to come to Earth and claim a huge success for my family and me and preferably not have you wiped out at the same time."

"Aye, that would be preferable. So, what happens now, then?"

"Well, unless you have a computer that I can use to hack into Hubble and send the message of gloatery, then we need to prepare to be smashed to smithereens."

"Really? Funny that, because we used to joke about being wiped out in a nuclear holocaust and how we would just about have time to boil an egg if the warning goes off. All these years on and I don't have any eggs. Actually, I might have eggs for my tea. Let's go to the village."

"You said you were going to have onions."

"I'm allowed to change my mind as the apocalypse arrives, aren't I? It's like having a wife telling me what I can and can't eat in my own house."

With the missiles about one hour away, Swamsoot and Tam Wilson walked along the clifftop path towards the village, arguing about liver or eggs for tea. Jack occasionally looked up at the sky because dogs just know when there's going to be bother.

Who Knew

Delius had taken on the look of a serious Bellsurpian as he began barking out messages without knowing if his skipper was dead or dying. *He just didn't know.*

Ethel knew what was needed to get Swamsoot to do his job correctly but couldn't be certain the messages were getting through to him. *She just didn't know.*

Bamber didn't know if his best friend would make it back in time for the pub on Friday night. *He just didn't know.*

The military men had fired the missiles and had started drawing up plans to salvage anything of value from the wreckage, but the atmospheric conditions around the planet Earth were a mystery, so they would need to engage the clever people in drawing up a strategy regarding how big the area to be covered would be or whether or not there would be any casualties. *They just didn't care.*

The Clever People Association had looked carefully at the data they had received from the military people and had started to compile some figures and had even taken the time to contemplate options, which was exactly the type of free thought the military frowned upon. This had led to some harsh words and, indeed, some surreptitious whispers, which in turn brought the Calistones into play. They, in turn, fed unhealthy thoughts to their kin which became a full-blown rumour based on nothing, which became bad dreams, albeit the type of dreams that could only happen when awake. Calistones had the fortunate ability to either sleep or not and performed equally well with or without. *They just didn't snore.*

Swamsoot and Tam had reached the shop and asked for eggs and liver but were distraught to find out they had neither. Tam complained and Swamsoot shrugged and each one couldn't understand the other's sentiment.

"If you were older, we could go to the pub," mentioned Tam Wilson

"I can look older if you want?"

"How do you do that?"

"I've made you a car and built you half a house without question, but you want to know if I can wear a false beard?" Seemed easy when he put it like that, so they went to the pub, where Tam explained they would drink together and not drink with anyone else. *They just didn't share.*

Guess What?

Milly looked at Swamsoot suspiciously as he sat talking to the island's grumpiest man.

"Where I come from, we are just the same as here, except everything is different."

Tam balked. "The same but different? What kind of gibberish is that?"

"I mean, we do the same as Earthlings by eating and drinking and some of us even sleep when we get tired. Many of the older Bellsurpians like to go out when the suns shine and lots of them talk about how things were thousands of years ago when they were kids."

"Thousands?"

"When they were kids. My best friend has a picture of a human on his bedroom wall wearing shorts and a striped shirt with thousands of humans watching him falling over. That's the type of obvious difference that I see between your planet and mine."

"You two are talking some rubbish from a very early stage." "This better not turn into something nasty, Tam Wilson," Milly noted loudly. "I won't be having any of that nonsense in here tonight."

Tam winked at his new mate. "Mind yer business, ye old goat."

"And that. There'll be none of that tonight from you or your friend, who you would think you would have had the decency to introduce, you bad-mannered heathen."

Swamsoot stood up and offered his hand. "Damalgo Winstonian Swamsoot, at your service."

"Damaddle, what now?"

"Damalgo Winstonian Swamsoot."

"Well, that is a strange name, young man. And what brings you to Scroat today and where are you from?"

"I am here from far away and could really do with the use of a computer, but Tam tells me there is no such device on your island because you are so far behind the known universe."

Milly folded her arms defensively. "I have a perfectly good computer here, I'll have you know, although that silly old duffer wouldn't know how to switch it on. You're more than welcome to use it if you need it for work or... something?"

"That's very kind of you," he said as he vaulted the bar counter and landed within kissing distance of the landlady. "Might I use it as a matter of urgency, please?"

"There it is," she said, pointing towards the small storage area adjacent to the bar. "The password is wossunderthekilt."

In one well-balanced movement, he sat at the computer, switched it on and inserted a drive with a malleable connection into the USB port and began typing frantically. Within a very short time, he returned to the bar and sat down next to Tam to take a drink from his glass.

"Everything ok, son?"

"Well," he started loudly and felt his volume reducing with each word. "It appears there are missiles about eighty-thousand thousand of your miles away heading to Earth and there's nothing we can do to stop it. Within, oh, I don't know, an hour or so, your planet will be blown apart with everyone and everything on it."

"I see," said Tam wistfully. "Do you want a drink of pop?"

Battleprop sat back in his seat and shouted at his servant. "Make sure those buttons are gleaming."

Nothing for Hours Then Two at Once Come Along

The card school had arrived. Eddie Fischwick, Billy McJack and Geordie Ticker were huddled around the table as Swamsoot began his explanation.

"What in God's name is the young feller talking about, Tam?" asked Eddie very early in the piece

"He's a Martian," Tam answered.

"No, I'm not. I'm Bellsurpian and proud of it. Martians are tiny little folk who are notoriously smelly. Sulphur, you see. And they're a little bit two-faced as well. My uncle Trungent was at a royal celebration on Lasfortinort a few years ago and when someone complained about the smell of sulphur, the Martians blamed him. Pungent Trungent, they called him, but never to his face. In fairness, they struggle to look anyone in the eye, but you get my point."

Geordie Ticker thought he understood. "Ah, you're a storyteller, son and not a bad one at that."

"Is this the one of the school trips you mentioned, Tam?" asked Billy on behalf of the Constabulary.

"That's what I assumed, Billy, but it turns out he's from outer space and not from the mainland at all."

"Outer space?" he enquired officially.

"Aye, outer space. I know what you're thinking, but he does some things…"

"Some things?" asked the normally quiet Geordie Ticker. "Bit Vague, Tam. What sort of things?"

"Things like…Just weird things that can't happen on Earth."

"Well, I've been to Soho in London and let me tell you…"

"No, Geordie, I mean things that you can't explain. Here, son. Do that thing with the cars."

Swamsoot was gazing through the window at the bright sunshine, trying to remember all of his basic training and how to face his own bereavement bravely. "Sorry?"

"That thing with the cars. Do it for the lads, will you?" he slowly stood up and walked to a table where a handful of magazines sat and carefully flipped through the pages until he found an automobile, waved his hand-held device at it, then sat down again.

"There you are, Tam. It's outside."

"Ha ha, wait until you lot see this," laughed the local agitator. "I've got a Ferrari and an Aston Martin at home." The four men walked swiftly to the door where they found the car park empty but for an old, black Vauxhall Vectra. "He must have parked it around the other side." The other side housed nothing of note, though and Tam suddenly felt exposed. "Here!" he shouted to Swamsoot, who was still sitting staring through the window when they re-entered. "Where's the car?"

"Erm, it's in the car park. Where else would you park a car? The keys are inside."

"You've lost your marbles if you're believing the storyteller, Tam, but he is a good storyteller," Eddie goaded him.

"Come on, son. Do the car thing for the lads otherwise, they'll never believe you." Swamsoot stood up and looked at the Vectra standing alone and pointed without words. "A Vectra? What's the point of that?"

"It's a car."

"But it's not a car… it's not a… Make another Ferrari for the lads. Come on, son. I need to show them something a bit special."

"But that's what is in the magazine."

Tam swept up the glossy publication and flicked furiously through the leaves until he found it. "Bugger," he said dejectedly. "Do you have any better magazines, Milly? These are full of puke."

"Tam Wilson!" she shouted. "Watch your language, or you'll be out on your ear."

"Sorry, hen. Do you have any other magazines, please? The boy needs to find something a bit better than a fifteen-year-old Vectra to make for the lads."

"All we have is what you see," she answered firmly as his friends began to giggle in a clear demonstration of disbelief. Tam turned page after page until he found an item to tick the box.

"Here, son. Can you do it with this?"

"Of course, I can, Tam. I'm not sure what you'll do with it, though?"

"Let me worry about that, son. You just do that thingymbobby thing that you do." Swamsoot shrugged and did the thingymbobby thing for Tam, who talked his friends into returning to the car park where the red, double-decker bus sat quietly waiting for passengers to climb aboard.

Just Listen, Will You?

Ethel was imploring General Battleprop without success. "But we don't know if the mission has been a success and if it has been, then you are destroying a planet for no good reason."

"Hang on; it's many gortanties away, but I won't throw you out for raising it," he reasoned unreasonably. "Because we won't be affected by its destruction.

"But we don't even know if our starship has left yet. You could be killing a significant amount of Bellsurpians, even if we have no idea how many are on board."

"But they are soldiers, so they are trained to die."

"No, they're not," answered the clever woman indignantly. "They're trained to kill, not to be killed."

"Tomatoe Tomato," he answered nonchalantly with limited knowledge of Earth speak. "I'll have you know that I am in line for a medal the size of a Gerndots left ear for this successful mission and I owe much of that success to Swamsoot's ability to die with dignity, so let's not think about what could be wrong with destroying a planet and let's celebrate the result."

"But if you destroy a planet with a Bellsurpian starship on it, you will be weakening your position within the known universe as well as losing the goodwill of the families whose relations will be lost to battle. All you need to do is press the self-destruct button, give them a little more time to complete the mission and start again. All you'll have lost is a couple of missiles." It made sense to him. It made perfect sense to her and that worried her. Clever people were renowned for understanding things. Anything the military understood generally confused them.

"I'll tell you what," he offered. "I will check with my PA and if my suit is back from the cleaners before tea time, I will press the self-destruct button. How's that?"

She scanned his comments for humour. None.

"Is that your best offer?"

"No," he replied sternly. "My best offer was not to throw you out for asking." Earth was doomed.

All four, including Milly, had been on the bus. Tam looked at Swamsoot like a proud father watching his son score for the school team for the first time.

"Told you," he said with a hint of arrogance.

"So, you're a spaceman, son?" Milly asked with an obvious level of bewilderment.

"I suppose so," he said quietly.

"And you can do things like that all of the time?" Geordie asked, pointing at the bus.

"Yes. Yes, I can."

"Not just buses, though?" Eddie requested.

"No, pretty much anything you have a picture of."

"So, you could get Tam a young wife?" Billy asked to the amusement of everyone except Tam.

"No living tissue," he responded dutifully.

Billy chanced his arm. "So, could you get us a few Land Rovers to get around the island?"

"I could, but you need to understand the gravity of the situation. There are missiles heading towards Earth that will destroy the planet and they could arrive any time now."

He hadn't said it particularly loudly but it boomed across the bar and left silence in its wake. They all looked initially at Tam, then back to Swamsoot, who avoided their gaze by staring apologetically at the floor.

"Can't you stop them?" asked Milly.

"Sorry," he said meekly. "No."

"So, we're doomed?" Billy said.

"Sorry, yes."

"No hope then?"

"Sorry, no."

A heavy pause followed. "Ok, can you knock us up a few sports cars? Milly can get a few pictures on that computer of hers and well, if we're all for the knacker's yard, we might as well have a bit of fun before we go?"

"Fair enough," Tam said in agreement. "Pointless scaring the rest of the world if there's nothing we can do about it. Let's have a look and see what cars we can have."

The spirits were suddenly high and the inevitable was just that. Just as suddenly and the way only humans can contemplate, they all made the decision to enjoy what little time they had left. They picked two more Ferraris from the computer screen, a Porsche and a Lamborghini and Milly decided two wheels would be her own taste and straddled a Harley Davison.

Swamsoot smiled as they all took off and he felt slightly aggrieved that the mission by default had been a complete success, but he was not going to be around to receive the plaudits.

Everything he had been told to do was happening before his eyes as the five old friends continually passed him on the one short road around the island on vehicles he could have easily sold to them days before without them ever needing them. Minds as passive as theirs simply needed the incentive to play on something they didn't need or want until it became a game, albeit an end game.

His mind drifted to Ethel and he wondered if she really liked him and whether she would be more upset to hear of his apparent mission failure or his failure to return. He thought of his parents and his youth and how he wished he could be home with them one last time to say everything that had to be said. The engines roared past him once again and he could hear the old locals screaming with joy each time they raced along the narrow road at break-neck speed. The wind breezed across his face from the engines and the air warmed up dramatically, almost sucking the oxygen out of the atmosphere and the truth suddenly hit him that this wasn't the engines of the cars. Nobody had trained him for this, so he didn't know what to expect; a flash of light perhaps or the flick of a switch, then darkness. What he heard was definitely not what he expected.

"Glad you're ok, sir," Delius said as he walked slowly down the ramp of the starship

"Delius. You're… here?"

"Yes, sir, and you are there."

"Indeed I am. I'm pleased to see you."

"Thank you, sir. We have your hand, sir, although you don't seem as dead as we were expecting."

He couldn't be bothered to ask. "No, I'm really not very dead at all, Delius." The situation suddenly came at him. "But we need to get away from here and…" Tam suddenly came past and sounded his horn and just as quickly was out of sight. "These people are going to die because we have allowed it, Delius."

"Have we, sir? Are they unwell?"

"No, they're not unwell, but they are about to be blown up and us with them if we don't get off this planet. What a shame. I've grown really quite fond of them in a very short space of time, but as military men, we need to do our duty, Delius. Bellsurp will soon destroy this planet and everything on it because we didn't get a message of gloatery back home quick enough and missiles are very close."

"Ah, about that, sir. We have sent a message back explaining that the missiles went somewhat astray."

Swamsoot looked at his first officer and considered what he had said but wondered about his capabilities with the command of the starship at his fingertips. He smiled knowingly.

"Did you manage to tap into the guidance system and alter the flight path or indeed destroy the missiles on route, Delius?"

"No, sir," he answered truthfully. "Whoever sent them was just a bad shot. They missed by a considerable distance and, as far as we are aware, are heading out towards the Gantrocker Galaxy. I hope they don't hit one of their outlanders because you know how angry they get?"

"They missed?"

"By a distance, sir."

The noise around the island was deafening and the residents came out to watch the gang known locally as 'the old duffers' tearing around the Isle of Scroat on very expensive machines. The Bellsurpians slipped quietly off home without saying goodbye and 'the old duffers' would forever be remembered for making up a story about a young boy and an apocalypse. Nobody believed them, of course

www.ingramcontent.com/pod-product-compliance
Lightning Source LLC
Chambersburg PA
CBHW070427170726
48291CB00002B/387